GALLIMAUFRY

SHORT-FORM FICTION, POETRY, HUMOR, AND ESSAYS

ELIZABETH BARTON

Compliation first published in the United States of America by Bartonia Publishing, Chicago, IL.

ISBN: 979-8-9880454-4-1

Book design, cover design, and cover images by Ian Barton.

Printed and distributed via Kindle Direct Publishing, a division of Amazon.

FOREWORD

On a summer evening not long after moving into our house in the Norwood Park neighborhood, on our way home from seeing the Cubs at Wrigley Field, we were heading north on Lincoln Avenue when Liz first spotted the sign and storefront for the Gallimaufry Gallery in Lincoln Square. "Oh, that's probably a fun little shop!" she exclaimed. When I asked what made her so certain, she proceeded to explain what gallimaufry meant and how she had long thought it was simply a great word. Since she was certainly a collector of fun, quirky words (and indie shops) her sentiment thus made perfect sense.

That moment quickly came to mind when I started to curate this work for publication. Like most serious writers she had ambitions to write the Great American Novel, but mostly she liked to *write*, eventually discovering—and becoming quite fond of—shorter formats. In particular, her discovery of the creative joys of flash fiction and microfiction helped ensure that she was almost continually writing *something*, developing ideas, seeking new outlets for sharing her stories with the world. It also resulted in a large collection of completed and in-progress works covering a broad range of format, style, and subject matter. A gallimaufry, indeed.

This collection is not intended to be any sort of "complete works" anthology of every short piece she ever wrote. I felt it best to allow her to serve as her own "editor" by only including those pieces that she herself submitted to one or more outlets for publication, so I am confident that she felt each one published herein to be worthy of release. Several dozen were in fact accepted and published (a few even *paid,* real cash money!), and a list of those publications is included at the end of this book.

While certain ideas do recur across the various stories, all products as they are of a single mind and creative spirit, each piece in this collection is a standalone work. I have made no attempt to organize them in a way that develops or emphasizes any aspect or idea in particular, except perhaps to illustrate the wide variety of concepts she was able to develop within each of the structural formats. My goal here was simply to ensure that those who have enjoyed her writing over the years have a single place to find all of the short-form pieces that she felt comfortable sharing with the world.

Ian Barton
Chicago, IL
March 2023

SHORT STORIES & FLASH FICTION

Being Alice

When I get to her room, she greets me, calling me Alice—her sister's name.

I'm Grace, her daughter.

I corrected her the first few times. That was before I understood—I am Alice in her reality, at least sometimes. There's no point in taking it personally when she doesn't remember me. It's not personal. It just is. Everyone is happier if I agree to be Alice.

So, I smile and call her Margie instead of Mom as I reach over and give her hand a quick squeeze hello. I sit down on the loveseat across from her recliner.

"Remember when we used to walk home from school together?" she says.

Clearly, she started reminiscing on her own before I arrived. "I do," I say. I don't, but I'm not me. I'm Alice. I've heard the stories enough to play along.

"You always wanted to take a shortcut," she says.

"Right. But you insisted on going the long way—past Tommy's house." I do my best to make it sound like the gentle teasing of a big sister.

She smiles. "I did have quite a crush on him." It's hard to tell in this lighting, but I think she might be blushing a little.

"I didn't mind," I say. "It was good exercise anyway."

She's still smiling as she looks toward the window, and I can tell she's not really seeing the maple leaves fluttering in the breeze. Instead, she's gazing into the past. "I wonder what ever happened to Tommy," she says.

I can tell that her crush never completely faded, and I wonder if there's anyone who could be Tommy the way that I'm Alice. That might be nice.

Closer to Free

I woke with a jolt. My heart raced, but my brain loped along as it reassembled the events of the previous day. I sat up in bed to take stock of myself. My lip was split, and my head hurt like hell, but apart from that, I was basically okay. I was in some cheap motel just off of the highway. The night before, I'd driven until I was so tired that I could hardly stay on the road, so I stopped here to crash. The clock on the bedside table said 10:38. Damn, had I ever crashed! I hadn't meant to sleep so long. I needed to get moving.

As I scrambled into my clothes from the previous day, I told myself to just stay cool and calm down. Everything was going to be all right if I just kept it together. If I panicked and rushed, I was bound to make stupid mistakes.

My stomach rumbled. I needed food. I hadn't eaten in more than 18 hours, and I wouldn't be worth a damn if I didn't get something into my system soon. Maybe some caffeine would knock this damn headache out too. After splashing my face with cold water and pulling my hair back into a ponytail, I grabbed my bag and headed to the diner across the parking lot from the motel.

As I sat sipping coffee, waiting for my breakfast, I pulled a map from my bag and examined it. The damn thing nearly covered the whole table, but I was stuck using an old-fashioned paper map since I'd ditched my iPhone. I couldn't risk using it. At worst, Joe would be able to track me if I kept it. Even if he didn't do that, he'd still be able to see records of my calls. Joe was smart and not easily out-foxed, so I certainly couldn't go leaving him blatant clues as to where I might be headed. Of course, that also meant that using credit cards was out. I had only one hundred fifty-five dollars that had to last me until I got to Louisa's place, which was about 500 miles away. From there on, she and the others in the network would be able to help. I knew only vaguely how it all worked, but that was the point. The less I knew about the process, the less likely it would be that Joe would find me. From what I was told, I knew that I'd be passed from one network member to another, each of them knowing only the step behind and the step in front of her. Eventually, I'd settle somewhere, hopefully safe and sound with a new identity.

I had my doubts. Part of me thought that Joe would find me no matter where I hid, but I had to keep telling myself that this would work. It had to. People even took their kids along when they did this, and it worked. I was by myself, so that had to be to my advantage. But had any of those other women had cops as boyfriends? I shook my head. Hell, this was my best shot at a normal life, if you could call it that. More normal than having the shit kicked out of me a couple times a week anyhow. More normal than reporting my boyfriend to the police, only to have them ignore me because he was one of them.

When it really came down to it, I was risking my life whether I stayed with Joe or made a run for it, so there was no reason not to go.

I drank more coffee and drummed my fingers on the table. I kind of wished that I smoked. There was something about this situation that seemed to call for a cigarette—as if I needed one more thing leading me to an early grave. If this were a scene in a movie, though, the heroin would definitely have a cig. I could just see it—the battered wife or girlfriend on the run, nervous and twitchy, sitting in a roadside diner, gulping down coffee and sucking on a menthol, substituting the minty smoke for sustenance. Ah, but all of that was going to change anyway. I'd start over and become the person I was supposed to be, not this strange woman who had been sucked into a situation that made her practically unrecognizable.

It's one of those things you think could never happen to you. You hear the stories about women whose boyfriends or husbands beat the shit out of them, and you think why don't they just leave? What the hell is wrong with them? Then, when it happens to you, you don't even recognize it as the same thing. You tell yourself that he's not like those other guys. He's really sorry. He actually didn't mean it. He'll change. By the time you realize he won't, you're in way over your head and begin thinking that you deserve to be hit for being such a dumbass and not walking out the door the second after he ever laid a hand on you. At least, that's how it was for me. I'm sure everyone has her own story, yet they're all sadly the same in so many ways. And no one can really understand unless it happens to her. I sure didn't.

"Here you go, hon," the waitress said with a smile as she set the plate of blueberry pancakes in front of me. "Can I get you anything else?"

I shook my head.

"Where ya headed?" she asked, tilting her head and motioning to the map, still partially unfolded on the table.

"Oh, you know. Here and there," I said, avoiding her gaze. I tried to look nonchalant as took the map off the table and folded it up the rest of the way. The waitress shrugged and walked away as I returned the map to my bag. I was being ultra-paranoid, of course. She had just been making conversation. This is what Joe had done to me—what I'd let him do to me.

I dug into my pancakes and finished them quickly. On the table, I left money to cover my meal, plus a tip that was probably more generous than I should give, considering my lack of funds. It was my apology for being rude.

Once I was back on the highway, I started to feel good again. Well, maybe not good, exactly, but better. Freer. Every dashed white line on the road that ticked by as I drove meant even more distance between Joe and me, and I was a little closer to having my life back. I rolled down the window and turned the radio up. I almost felt good enough to laugh when "Bad Romance" by Lady Gaga came on. How apropos. I knew a thing or two about band romances, that was for sure. I think I lost myself for a few seconds singing along, "Rah, rah, romama. Gaga ooh lala," because the next thing I knew, there were red and blue lights in my rearview mirror. The music was too loud for me to hear the sirens. I glanced down to see that my speed was eighty-five.

Fuck. If I got a ticket, it would be in the system, and that would give Joe a lead on where I was. Could I outrun the cop? Probably not in this old heap. And if I tried and failed, I'd be in even deeper shit, and Joe would definitely know where I was.

Damn. It probably didn't matter anyway because the cop was now close enough to have gotten a look at my plates for sure. Stupid, stupid, stupid. I cursed myself as I pulled over and slowed the car. How could I be so careless?

I killed the engine, and before I could even think of how I was going to plead with the officer to get out of this, the police car whizzed by me. He was after someone else.

I realized I had been holding my breath and let it out. I sat there, just breathing for until I stopped shaking. Slow down. Stay cool, and take it easy. When I restarted the car, "Closer to Free" by the BoDeans roared to life on the radio.

The Committee

While Shirley Jackson's The Lottery was a fictionalized account, the story was inspired by true events that persist to this day.
—Michaela Hutchinson, American Historian

The mood in the room was decidedly less festive than that suggested by the selection of snacks and beverages laid out. Instead of refreshments for four people, it looked more like a party spread for a dozen or more guests. As host, Janice Jones had taken the opportunity to try out a few new recipes. Polenta puffs with homemade creamy tomato goat cheese dipping sauce, graham cracker crostini topped with brie and lavender honey, and cinnamon brownies with a hint of cayenne pepper were among the offerings.

The task ahead of them had apparently not dampened the appetite of Paul Warner, who'd taken at least three of everything, stacking the victuals on a small appetizer plate in a pile that looked precarious enough to evoke anxiety from Melanie Allen. Her eyes fixed on Paul as he lumbered to the table. When he arrived at his place, he put his plate down without spilling a morsel, and Melanie exhaled.

Gary Summers eyed Paul's heap of snacks. "Geez, Paul. Did you skip lunch?"

Paul shrugged. Janice waved her hand in dismissal. "Oh, please! There's plenty! Take as much as you like!"

Paul looked at Gary with a tiny smile of vindication on his lips. Gary said nothing but wore a look of uninterest.

"You didn't need to go to all this trouble. We're here for town business, not to eat." Melanie looked uncomfortably stiff in her seat at the dining room table. "In fact, I think after this year we should go back to holding these meetings in a conference room at the Town Hall instead of people's homes."

Janice looked hurt. "I know none of us want to be here. I was only trying to make this unpleasantness a little less unpleasant."

"Yeah," said Paul. "I think it's much nicer this way." He bit into a toast point topped with olive tapenade. "Mmmph, Janice, this is so good."

Janice smiled and folded her hands on the table. "Thank you."

Melanie softened. "I don't mean any offense. I just think this should feel less like a casual get-together and more official. That way, we can get this done as efficiently as possible."

"I'm all for efficiency, but there's no harm in having a little snack. Isn't it better not to make important decisions on an empty stomach?" Janice looked expectantly toward Melanie, and after a beat, Paul and Gary turned their eyes toward her as well.

Melanie's eyes darted among the three faces. "Fine," she said, pushing her chair away from the table and rising to her feet.

Janice watched with a look of satisfaction as Melanie picked up a plate. "Is everyone OK on drinks? Aside from the water and sparkling pomegranate lemonade," she said, gesturing toward the pitchers at one end of the sideboard, "There's coffee in the kitchen, which should be done brewing any minute. I could put some water on for tea. I've got English Breakfast, green, and a few different herbal teas—chamomile, mint, ginger-peach, and…" She ticked off the varieties on her fingers, the nails of which were short, neat, and painted with pearl-colored polish.

"I think we're good," Gary said.

Melanie returned to the table with her plate, which held a few grape tomatoes and some hummus. She retook her seat. "Now I think we can get started, yes?"

"Orange blossom!" said Janice.

Melanie turned toward Janice. "What?"

"It's the last type of herbal tea I couldn't remember," Janice said.

"Great," said Melanie. Her look of weary exasperation suggested she was using most of her might to suppress an eye roll. "But as Gary said, I think we're good."

"I'd drink some orange blossom tea," said Paul.

"Sure!" Janice sprung to her feet. "It will just take a moment. I'll put the kettle on." She hurried to the adjacent kitchen.

Melanie glared at Paul. "Seriously?"

Paul shrugged. "I like orange blossom."

Gary looked from Melanie to Paul and back again. "It's fine. Another couple of minutes isn't going to kill anyone."

Melanie winced ever so slightly.

"Yeah," said Paul. He half-stifled a snicker. "That's our job."

"Is that supposed to be funny?" The look Melanie directed toward Paul brimmed with disapproval.

Paul's face fell. "I…uh. No…I just mean…" His stammering trailed off, leaving a moment of silence its wake.

"Don't worry about it," Gary said. "I don't think there's anything wrong with a bit of gallows humor in the face of what we have to do."

"Well, I don't appreciate it," Melanie said.

Gary sighed. "Listen, this is my fourth year—my last year—on the Committee, so I think I know what I'm talking about when I say that people deal with this in different ways. Janice, apparently, makes a shit-ton of food. Paul eats a shit-ton of food and makes grim jokes."

"Gary mansplains to the Committee Chair," said Melanie.

"Touché," Gary said with a smile, holding up his hands in surrender. "All I mean is that you've got to let people cope how they need to."

"I know, but that can be hard when different people have opposite strategies. Some people want to start—and therefore get finished—as soon as possible. Some people..." Melanie motioned toward the kitchen with a tilt of her head. "...seem to prefer avoidance tactics."

From the kitchen, the whistle of a tea kettle began quietly, grew in volume until it reached a shrill shout, then faded. Moments later, Janice re-entered the dining room carrying a steaming teacup on a saucer—understated and elegant, classic white porcelain with a gold vine pattern encircling the cup about two-thirds of the way from the bottom. She placed the cup in front of Paul. "Here you go."

"Thanks." Paul reached for the teabag and tugged on its string, making it bob up and down in its bath.

"You're welcome," said Janice. "Can I get anyone anything else?"

"No, thank you, Janice." Melanie's smile looked forced. "It was so nice of you to provide all the food and drinks, but I think we're ready to get down to business."

Janice's lips remained upturned, but the smile faded from her eyes. "Yes. All right then," she said softly as she returned to her seat at the table.

Melanie opened the manila folder in front of her. "First, we need to select a new Committee member to take Gary's place next year. I put a list of the eligible candidates in each of your folders."

Janice, Paul, and Gary opened the folders at their places and looked down at the first page within.

"Wow." Janice furrowed her brow and paged ahead to see how long the list went on. "There sure are a lot of names. Are they in any sort of order?"

"No," Gary said. "That's done on purpose. The list used to be alphabetized, but the Committee usually just picked the first person on it. Now, a computer randomizes the names to make it fair."

"Oh," said Janice. "Does that mean we should just pick the first name on the list?"

Gary shrugged. "Unless someone can come up with a good reason not to. It's what we've done in the past. It makes our lives easier."

Paul frowned at the paper in front of him and raised a finger. "I'm not in favor of that."

"Why's that?" said Gary.

"The first person on the list is my mother-in-law. Doesn't that create a conflict of interest or something?"

"I don't see how," said Gary. "We're not talking about picking her...to be the designee. I don't see why it would be a problem to pick her as a Committee member."

Melanie tapped her pen on the paper. "Actually, I think Paul has a point." Paul straightened up in his chair, looking surprised but pleased. "Having two Committee members related to one another—that could be seen as one family exerting undue influence on Committee decisions."

"Well, my mother-in-law and I almost never agree on anything," Paul offered.

"That could still be problematic," said Melanie. "If the two of you are going to do nothing but clash, that could gum up the works."

Gary waggled his head from side to side, then slowly brought it to the center and started to nod. "Yeah, I guess I see your point. What do you think, Janice?"

"That sounds reasonable. If we want to skip Paul's mother-in-law, that's fine with me."

"OK," Gary said. "The next name on the list is Aubrey Simmons. Anyone have any objections to her?"

The table was quiet as the Committee members considered the question.

Janice cleared her throat. "I don't know her, so I have no objection."

"Yeah, same here," said Paul.

Everyone looked toward Melanie, who pursed her lips and sighed through her nose. "I've met her, but I don't know her well enough for anyone to see it as a conflict of interest. No objections here."

"All right. That settles that," Gary said.

Melanie was already neatly printing on her notepad to record the decision. "Now," she said. She stopped writing but kept her eyes fixed on the papers in front of her. She swallowed audibly and started again. "Now for the main matter of our meeting. I've put the list of eligible designee candidates in your folders as well."

Papers rustled as the Committee members paged forward. This list was shorter than the previous one but still filled two pages.

"Forgive me," Janice said. "This might be a dumb question, but I'm newest on the Committee, so I have a lot to learn...How do you choose? What have you done in the past, and where does this list come from in the first place?"

"From a computer," Gary explained. "The names of all town residents are fed in, and an algorithm narrows things down to a more manageable list of choices."

"But how does the algorithm do that?" Janice fingered the thin gold chain around her neck, idly twisting it as she spoke. "What is it based on? And who created it?"

"No one knows," said Paul. "Before the town transitioned from the old way of doing things, several programmers submitted algorithms for potential use. All of them were screened by a panel of knowledgeable town residents, and ones that were deemed unsuitable were scrapped."

"OK," said Janice, "but they obviously had to pick one, so someone had to know which one it was."

"I was getting to that," Paul said. "The algorithms were submitted during the last year the lottery system was used. The idea was to start using the algorithm the following year. So, when the designee was identified that final year of the lottery, their final act was to choose the algorithm that would be used from that point forward. So, they're the only one who knew, and the secret died with them."

Janice blinked rapidly as she processed this information. "I see," she said, although it wasn't clear if she really did.

"That's what they say anyway," Melanie said. "I have a hard time believing that no one knows. That was more than 40 years ago, and if nothing else, there have been so many technological advances since then. I'd think someone would have figured out ways around the security features that were put in place back then."

Paul shook his head. "I don't know about that. They say the program was supposed to self-destruct if any kind of tampering was detected. That would mean no more algorithm, and we'd have to go back to the old way of doing things, at least for a while."

"If someone could figure out how to tamper with it, I'm guessing they could also find a way to circumvent the self-destruction command," said Janice.

Paul shrugged. "Maybe, but I've heard it's all quite sophisticated, especially considering when it was created. The town government brought in outside people to get everything set up and paid a lot of money to do so—we're talking top people in their fields at the time."

"Of course, all of this is assuming you believe town lore," said Gary.

Paul seemed to take offense. "You don't?"

"I think things get exaggerated when rumors get going," Gary said, "especially when there's mystery and controversy around the topic to begin with."

For a second, Paul looked like he might argue further, but he didn't, and a lull fell across the table.

"I guess what I don't understand," Janice began, "is why the town stopped doing things the old way. Switching to the system we use now…well, it puts an awful lot of pressure on the Committee, don't you think?"

Melanie nodded. "Yes, of course there's pressure. That's by design. No one should take this lightly. The old way was too arbitrary."

"But couldn't you argue that since it was so arbitrary, it was actually the only way it could be completely fair?" said Janice.

"I've heard there were concerns about the lottery being rigged," said Paul.

"How could it have been rigged?" Gary asked. "Everyone in town was there to watch the whole thing happen."

"Sleight of hand. Distraction techniques," said Paul. "Think about so-called magicians. Everyone knows there's no such thing as magic, but there are plenty of magicians who are good enough to almost make you believe magic is real because their tricks are so good."

"I've always heard that the town had just gotten too big to continue doing it the old way. The lottery was fine back when there were 300 people in the town, but once the population started growing, it was all taking too long," said Gary.

"Well, that makes sense," said Janice. "But why create the Committee? Why not have the algorithm do the choosing?"

"I think people wanted a human check," Gary said. "Rumors of rigging aside, the lottery was fair, and people trusted it because they could see it happening. I think a lot of people didn't trust a mysterious algorithm to make a fair choice—or they thought that the algorithm was actually BS and there was just one person behind the scenes choosing the designee. The Committee added a layer of human involvement and some accountability."

"Regardless," said Melanie, jumping in before anyone else could take the current line of conversation further, "we don't use the old system now, so it's a moot point. We should get back to the task at hand."

The rest of the group seemed resigned to follow Melanie's instruction as their eyes returned to the document in front of them.

"I know none of us relish this task," Melanie said, "And we may not know all the factors that went into the algorithm to generate this list, but if you look back at the designees who've been chosen since this system was put in place, I think it's safe to say that the algorithm favors those who are less-than-optimal citizens."

"That's true," said Paul. "There hasn't been a single designee who didn't have at least some criminal record since we started using the current system. And no kids have been designees either."

Janice shuddered. "I can hardly believe kids could be designees with the old lottery system."

"It was a different time," said Paul.

Janice shot him a skeptical frown.

"I don't mean that people didn't love their kids," said Paul. "It's just that people weren't quite so precious about childhood back then."

"I might understand that if you were talking about a really long time ago," Janice said, "but child labor laws started—when? Like the 1930s? The lottery system was around way beyond that."

"Regardless," Melanie said. "We've got the algorithm now, which seems to have fixed that particular problem."

Janice slouched in her chair, an act that seemed to be done not out of sloppiness, but rather to make herself look smaller. "What concerns me," she said, "is that this algorithm is a black box. It might be unfairly targeting certain groups of people. We have no way of knowing because we don't have any clue how it works."

"So, you think criminals are an unfairly targeted group?" Paul jeered, as if the very idea was absurd.

Janice straightened up. "Well, maybe. Consider the things that drive people to crime: desperation, poverty. Plus, when I think about the systemic racism and sexism that persist in society today, it hardly makes me confident that an algorithm developed—when was it? The late 70s? the early 80s?—doesn't have those biases built right into it."

The rest of the group stared at Janice with expressions that suggested they were seeing her in a new way. Her outward appearance, especially when combined with the impressive spread of refreshments, evoked an image-conscious woman—one who wanted to foster the impression of a picture-perfect life, not necessarily one who spent a lot of time cogitating on issues of social justice.

After a lengthy silence, Melanie was first to speak. "Well, Janice, that's a very good point." She jiggled the pen in her hand in a frenetic rhythm. "Does anyone have suggestions as to how we might address that?"

"I think the best way would be to make sure the designee isn't from a marginalized group," said Janice. She glanced down at the list. "After just a quick scan, it looks like that would eliminate…um, I mean…rule out a lot of people."

Gary frowned down at the list. "She's right. I mean, obviously, our town has some diversity, but it looks like minorities are over-represented on this list. As far as I can tell, way more than half the people on here are part of some minority group. Yet, look at all of us on the Committee—all white."

Paul frowned and let a sigh escape from his lips. "Listen, you might be right about the list being somewhat skewed, but I don't see why being a minority should automatically get you out of being the designee."

Melanie rolled her eyes. "Of course, you don't. You're a straight, white, cis-gendered, middle-class man."

Paul blinked at her. "And?"

Gary snorted. "Geez, Paul. I'm hardly the most woke man in the world, but even I'm able to recognize at least some of my privilege."

Paul scoffed. "You guys think I'm privileged? I've worked hard for everything I have!"

"No one is saying you didn't," Janice said gently. "It's just that, all other things being equal, you would have had to work even harder for exactly the same things if you were a person of color."

"Or a woman. Or gay," Melanie added.

Paul looked at each of his fellow Committee members. He seemed to be searching their faces for some hint of solidarity but not finding it. "I'm not going to sit here and debate who worked hardest for what. I was just posing the question of whether being a minority should earn you a free pass."

"Well, I think the rest of us agree that, in most cases, it probably should," said Janice. She looked to Melanie and Gary, who nodded reassurance.

"Fine," Paul muttered. "Who does that leave us with?"

"Let's see," said Melanie. She started at the top of the list and placed an X next to the first six names. "Marshall Walker?"

"No. He's gay," said Janice.

"He is?" Paul raised his eyebrows.

"Oh, that's right. I forgot," said Melanie.

The rest of the Committee members looked at Paul, almost like they were daring him to voice some sort of issue. When he said nothing, Melanie placed an X next to Marshall's name and continued down the list. "Amanda Delacroix?"

The Committee members looked at one another, exchanging silent shrugs.

"OK, then. She's a possibility." Melanie continued down the list, placing an X next to three more names before reaching the next candidate who wasn't a member of a marginalized group as far as anyone knew.

Once they'd gone through the entire algorithm-generated list in this manner, only nine names without Xs remained: Amanda Delacroix, Bill Barclay, Andy Miller, Gretchen Dunbar, Doug Martin, Joe Langman, Susan Maguire, Albert Bentham, and Rory Stevens.

"How should we choose from who's left?" Paul asked.

"This is the part I've been dreading. I know it needs to be done, but..." Janice left her sentence unfinished, leaving everyone at the table to fill in the blank.

Another silence fell. Each Committee member appeared pensive. Perhaps they were thinking of all the ways they might complete Janice's unfinished sentence. Maybe they were questioning whether this task actually needed to be done, and if so, why? Tradition? As a stark memento mori for the entire town? To remind people of the value of life? To ensure prosperity? Once upon a time, there had been a saying: Lottery in June, corn be heavy soon. But farming had ceased to be a major industry in the town decades ago, so one could no longer claim that the sacrifice was done to ensure a bountiful harvest. Still, it was hard to deny that their town had been prosperous, its growth far outpacing that of many other towns in the area—ones that had long ago dispensed with this particular tradition.

As they sat with their thoughts, each Committee member at some point seemed on the verge of speaking. Perhaps one or more was on the precipice of voicing their questions: Do we really have to do this? Can we simply choose not to?

But if those thoughts were on the tongues of the Committee members, they were not released. They remained unsaid, trapped inside mouths and stifled into nothingness.

Gary broke the long silence. "We could put all the names in a hat and draw one at random."

The others at the table gave slow nods of agreement.

"That would probably be the fairest way," said Janice.

"I suppose that's true." There was little conviction behind Melanie's voice.

"Overall, I think this is an improvement over the old way. The algorithm generated the initial list, and we spared the minorities," Janice offered with a similar paucity of confidence.

"Agreed," said Gary.

"I'm OK with it," said Paul. Most of the food he'd taken earlier remained on his plate, uneaten.

"All right then," said Melanie. She began to write the names on a piece of paper. For each name, she tore off a strip off from the sheet. Gary took each strip and folded it up, making them all look roughly identical.

"Who's going to pick?" Paul asked as Gary pushed the pieces of paper to the center of the table and stirred them around.

"I have an idea," Janice said. "There are nine slips of paper and four of us. What if we each pick two from the pile and the one that's left will be the designee? That way, no one will have it on their conscience that they chose the designee."

Melanie looked impressed. "That's a good idea."

Gary and Paul nodded.

"OK." Melanie reached for the center of the table and took a slip of paper.

Gary, Paul, and Janice followed suit, each taking a slip for themselves. Melanie picked another slip. Gary and Paul did the same.

Janice reached. Her hand hovered as she considered the final two pieces of paper. She closed her eyes and took a deep breath. Her fingers chose the final slip and curled around it.

Dinner for Two

"Sweetie, I'm home," she called, stomping the snow from her feet. "Man, it is not pleasant out there." She unwound the scarf from her nick, shed her coat, and sat down on the bench in the entryway to remove her boots. "Count yourself lucky that you got to work from home today!" She stood again and shivered against the cold she'd brought inside with her. Rubbing her arms, she padded toward the living room. "How was your day?"

Her question was met with silence. The living room was empty, which meant he was still in their home office. Ugh. Working from home was nice and all, but if he was still at it after seven o'clock on a Friday, that didn't bode well for his mood. "Bad day, huh?" She directed her voice toward the office. "Do you want to talk about it?" She always asked, even though she knew he didn't. Whenever he was in a bad mood, he became taciturn. It probably wasn't healthy for him to bottle things up, but what could she do? Trying to drag things out of him only increased his grumpiness exponentially.

She paused before the mirror in the hallway and ran her fingers through the ends of her hair, working through the damp snarls crafted by the wind and snow. "Maybe someone needs a back rub." She knew he could hear her, and although he didn't respond, she sensed a mood shift. Back rubs were her not-so-secret weapon. Sometimes she daydreamed about quitting the rat race and going to massage therapy school. Each time she saw his tension evaporate as a lazy smile found its way onto his lips while she kneaded his muscles, she wondered if massage was her true calling.

"I'll tell you what," she said, "I'm going to head upstairs and change. Then I'll order Thai and open a bottle of wine." She trotted upstairs, not waiting for a reply. She might have to drag him out of the office, but he'd thank her for it later. Sometimes he got so fixated on a problem that he couldn't pry himself away. On some level, he had to know what he really needed was a break and some distance so he could later return to the problem with a fresh perspective. But, knowing and doing were two different things. She was happy to be the enforcer of break time if that's what he needed.

She exchanged her work clothes for a sweatshirt, yoga pants, and slippers. As she pulled her hair back into a ponytail, she smiled at the wedding picture on her dresser. Had that really been almost nine years ago? In many ways, it seemed like just yesterday, but the impossibly young, fresh faces in the photo reminded her that there had been a whole lot of yesterdays between then and now. But it was good. Sure, all that time had given them both some grey hairs and lines around their eyes, but it had also brought a greater richness and depth to their relationship. Compared with back then, there were fewer thrills and surprises now, but there was a lot to be said for comfort and reliability. She'd never understood when people talked about marriage as being hard work. It had never felt that way to her. Somehow, the way they balanced each other out made everything seem easier.

She went back downstairs to the kitchen. With a few taps on her phone, she placed their usual order from Thai Table—spring rolls, red curry chicken for him, and Siam tofu for her.

With that done, she grabbed a bottle of white wine from the fridge and a corkscrew from the nearby drawer. As she opened the bottle, she realized she was humming—Moonlight Serenade. She'd always thought the tune had such a dreamy quality. She smiled and filled two glasses with the straw-colored liquid. "OK," she said as carried them into the living room, finding it still empty. "Dinner is on the way, and I've got wine." She walked toward the office and stopped just outside the door. With both her hands holding wine glasses, she couldn't open it, but that was fine. If she opened it, she'd face undeniable proof that he wasn't in there. If the door remained shut, she could go on pretending, at least for a little longer. What was the harm in that? She closed her eyes and sighed, leaning her forehead heavily into the wooden door. "I miss you," she whispered, hoping he could somehow hear her and that he already knew.

Down There

From up on the ledge, everything looked serene—well, maybe not serene exactly, but at least orderly. There was plenty if activity. Cars drove by, people moved to and fro, and the traffic lights kept a rhythmic balance to it all. From up there, the world looked like a place that Ned could live in and maybe even be happy in. But the view from the ledge was deceptively different than the experience of actually being down there in the midst of it all.

From up high, you could look out at the city, and you would never believe that little girls died in their cribs at night without reason or warning. Up there, Ned could almost forget that his wife cringed at his touch because it only reminded her of the sadness. No, the world looked neat and purposeful, like he was watching little parts of some great machine.

Ned was only 27 floors up, and he wondered what the world would look like and what he could forget about if he went even higher—a mountaintop, an airplane, a spacecraft. He had seen pictures of the Earth taken from space. How lovely and peaceful the planet looked from up there! How could it be that people on that pretty blue orb were dying in wars, lying, raping, cheating, stealing, manipulating, and murdering?

Perhaps God, if He existed at all, was just too far away to notice. Maybe with a God's eye view, everything seemed just fine. Couldn't God be bothered to take a closer look every once in a while to make sure that little babies kept on breathing while they slept? If He couldn't even do that, what good was He? What good was anything?

Ned's cell phone vibrated in his pocket. His boss was probably calling, wondering why he hadn't shown up at the team meeting. No one had yet realized Ned was up here. He let the call go to voicemail as he considered his options: get off of the ledge, go back inside, and make up some excuse for being late to the meeting; or step off the ledge and show God and everyone else just what he thought of this harsh, chaotic world.

But for the moment, he was just going to enjoy the view.

Duped

"Stop right there."

Jada froze. The voice was familiar yet sounded slightly off—like a recording of herself. She turned her head to see the gun pointed at her.

A gun! Jada despised guns, and the fact that Jada-2 was wielding one served as further proof that the device could not be allowed to remain in existence. Already, it had created such chaos—and she'd had only purest of intentions when in building it. She shuddered to think of what might ensue if it fell into the wrong hands.

"Let go of the device and step back."

Jada, still poised with both hands inside the safe, remained motionless. "You know I can't do that."

"You can and you will," said Jada-2.

"Or what? You'll shoot me?" Jada shifted her focus from the gun barrel and looked into Jada-2's eyes, identical to those she'd seen in the mirror thousands of times, narrowed at her in anger. "I don't think you'll do that."

"Oh? Why is that?"

"Because you have no idea what will happen. It might very well be as if you shot yourself. Essentially, you are me." Jada didn't know what would happen either. They were in uncharted territory, but planting this seed of fear was her best strategy.

"True, there's a chance that killing you would also kill me," said Jada-2, "but you forget that I know everything you knew right up until the time of the split. I know you built in a kind of rewind mechanism—the decoherence pulse, and that will definitely kill me. So, if I need to, I'll take my chances with shooting you."

Jada wasn't sure whether the decoherence pulse would even work. The split that created Jada-2 had occurred when the device was activated. In theory, the decoherence pulse would reverse that process, causing Jada-2 to collapse back into Jada. But none of this had ever been done before. The outcome was far from certain.

Things used to be so simple—as simple as quantum physics can be anyhow. Certainly, everything was much less complicated back when it was all theoretical. When Jada had begun working on the device, she'd had little confidence it would actually work. Expanding the quantum realm to the macroscopic level, allowing for human superpositioning—it seemed altogether fantastic. If she'd thought it really would work, perhaps she'd have pondered the potential consequences more carefully. She'd mused about how useful it would be to literally be in two places at once. She hadn't considered that doing so would mean using twice the resources she once had. That wasn't hugely problematic for a single person, but if the technology got out, it could essentially create a population explosion overnight, one that could be multiplied again and again. The planet could never sustain it.

What's more, Jada had figured her twin would be just like her. Instead, Jada-2 was more like a proverbial evil twin—at least that's what Jada told herself. What she didn't like to admit was that everything inside of Jada-2 was also inside of her. If Jada had no responsibilities, no concerns of being held accountable for anything (since it would all fall back on a look-alike), would she act just as reckless as Jada-2 had? She didn't want to think so, but whatever was driving Jada-2 had come from somewhere, and in this case, somewhere meant the dark parts of Jada's mind that she'd learned to keep hidden.

"It's true," Jada said. "I created the decoherence pulse mechanism in case something went wrong. But I wasn't intending to use it now. All I want to do now is destroy this thing and my files so no one can re-create it."

Jada-2 scoffed. "Am I really so bad that I make you want to destroy one of the greatest-ever technological advances?"

Jada swallowed hard and tried to make her voice sound steady, sincere. "It's not you. It's the thought of millions, if not billions of people creating their own splits. You must see how that would be mayhem!"

Jada-2 seemed to soften ever so slightly. "Still, why should I believe you won't use the decoherence pulse before you destroy the device? I've caused you quite a bit of trouble."

In under two weeks, Jada-2 had gotten Jada accused of cheating on her husband, maxed out three of her credit cards, received two speeding tickets, and, judging by the cold looks and whispers that had been following her lately, caused some havoc Jada had yet to discover. "I won't deny that. But destroying you would be murder. You know me—you practically are me. I may be a lot of things, but I'm not a murderer."

Jada-2 didn't appear to be buying it. "I'm going to count to three," she said. "One."

Jada's mind grabbled for another plan but came up short.

"Two."

"OK!" Jada said. If she could buy herself more time, maybe she could still talk her way out of this. "I'm going to back away—slowly. I don't want to startle someone with a gun pointed at me."

"Good girl," said Jada-2.

As Jada backed away from the safe, an alarm beeped an alert that the door had been open for more than two minutes. Seeing Jada-2's distraction at the noise, Jada lunged for the gun, but Jada-2 jerked away and fired.

The bullet missed Jada and went into the safe. The sound of a buzz swelled and receded, leaving in its wake two more duplicates—one each for Jada and Jada-2. Each Jada looked at the others, bewildered.

"What's happening?!" Jada-2 shouted.

"Another split," said Jada. Before she finished speaking, the buzzing sound pulsed again and there were eight Jadas. Shit. "Shoot them!" Jada shouted at Jada-2.

"What? Why?"

"If the doubling continues, there will be over two billion in five minutes!"

As Jada-2 absorbed this information, there was another split. The Jada-2 doubles all raised their guns, probing the room with wild, darting eyes, seemingly unsure of where to aim their shots.

Fated

Amid the calliope music that permeated the air, my eager eyes feasted on the spectacle around me. From the high striker and the ring toss to the towering Ferris wheel, it was almost too magnificent to take in at once. The carnival's arrival in Sublette was the most excitement a 10-year-old Kansas farm girl could hope for. And judging from the crowd, folks from all over Haskell County shared my enthusiasm.

I was itching to ride The Whip. My kid brother Tommy had his heart set on a visit with Madame Delphia, the fortune-teller. He insisted she wasn't like all those fakes out there. She was the genuine article with the gift of second sight. I don't know how he knew this, but he seemed so sure of it—I wasn't going to argue and spoil his fun. For all I knew, he might be right.

"There!" Tommy pointed. He tugged at the sleeve of Mama's dress, pulling her toward the crimson tent fringed with gold.

"Waste of money if you ask me," Pop muttered, shaking his head.

Mama smirked, dismissing him with a wave of her hand. "It's just a bit of fun. What's the harm."

Pop shrugged in acquiescence.

As we arrived at the threshold of Madame Delphia's lair, hints of trepidation crept onto Tommy's face, mingling there with his excitement. "Come in with me, Mama?"

Mama smiled down at him. "Sure."

The two of them stepped forward. Tommy fished a hand into his pocket, then proudly handed his coins to the tent tender. He and Mama clasped hands and disappeared through the tent flaps.

#

By the time they re-emerged, I was well into my cone of cotton candy, relishing each luscious moment as it melted on my tongue. I was about to tease Tommy—telling him I'd gotten the last one and they were all out now, but I saw his cheeks were streaked with tears.

"What'd she say?" I asked.

Tommy clutched at Mama's side and buried his face in the fabric of her dress, silent in his tearful anguish.

I looked to Mama. Her face was ashen. "What'd she say?"

"Plague," Mama murmured, her eyes wide but unfocused. "All of us…dead within a year."

"Plague!" Pop scoffed. "It's 1917, not the Dark Ages! What nonsense!"

Fledgling

When Ava was young and people asked her what she wanted to be when she grew up, she always responded the same way: "A bird."

Adults would smile and chuckle, often commenting on how cute, how precious her answer was. A few of them pressed her further. "No, really," they'd say after laughing off the initial answer.

Ava's face would go all pensive, making the adults think she was going to answer seriously this time. But eventually, she'd say something like, "An owl, I think. Or maybe an eagle."

When she was 14, she started to dye her hair. Bright hues of yellow, green, blue, and red mimicked vivid avian plumage. The colors evoked more parrot than owl or eagle, but that was OK. She still hadn't figured out exactly what type of bird she would be.

When she was 17, she got a fake ID. Unlike many kids her age who used theirs to buy beer, Ava took hers straight to a tattoo parlor. During several sessions, she sat patiently through hours of discomfort as the artist rendered feathers that began at her shoulder blades, arched out over the backs of her shoulders, and tapered off near the middle of her upper arm.

Around the time she turned 18, her nose started to take on a more beak-like appearance, becoming subtly but noticeably longer and narrower. People wondered and whispered behind her back. Had she gotten a nose job? She had not.

Then, her skin began to change. Tiny bumps arose on its surface, barely perceptible at first, eventually resembling a constant case of gooseflesh. Most everyone assumed she was one of those people who was cold all the time, and she started to dress the part, wearing long pants and sleeves. She weathered all this without complaint. It was merely an awkward phase. She'd get through it.

In early spring, the year she turned 19, she lay in her bed one night, wrestling with an irksome sleeplessness. Usually, she had no trouble drifting off and slumbering soundly through the night. But that evening, the longer she lay there waiting for languor to envelope her, the more alert she felt. Unable to be still any longer, she rose from her bed and went to the window. Looking out over the moonlit back yard below, she suddenly knew why sleep would not come. The time to fulfill her destiny was at hand.

She left her bedroom and descended the stairs, her bare feet stepping lightly, avoiding the creaky spot on the stair halfway down, so as not to disturb the rest of her family. She slipped out the back door and into the yard. For a moment she worried that she wouldn't know what to do, but she soon found the knowledge she needed. Whether it had come from an external source or had emerged from somewhere deep within her after a long dormancy, she could not discern. But there it was, flowing through her brain.

Stepping barefoot onto the cool, damp carpet of grass, she moved toward the hammock that stretched between the two old maple trees on the east side of the yard. She unhooked each end, rolled and folded the web-like fabric, slung it over her shoulder, and walked with a purposeful grace to the large oak near the south end of the yard. There, she found an easily accessible branch that would support her weight. Grabbing hold of the tree limb, she pressed her feet against the furrowed trunk and hoisted herself up. Ascending as she moved from bough to bough, she searched until she found the right spot: the perfect crook where three thick branches diverged. Perching on a branch, holding tight with her thighs, she took the hammock in her hands, twisting and sculpting it into a circular bedstead. When she had arranged it just so, she situated herself in the center and settled in.

She felt something stirring in her chest—a sort of fluttering, part nervousness, part exhilaration. This was her destiny. She could hardly remember not knowing that, but the exact pathway to it had never been clear. So, it was scary, setting off into the unknown like this, even though her destination felt like the place she was meant to be.

It was the transformation that worried her more than anything else. Would it hurt? Would she feel something akin to growing pains, or would she simply fall asleep and awake fully transformed? And when it was over, how much would she remember? She wasn't too concerned about forgetting the transformation process. If it was painful, it might be best forgotten. But she feared forgetting the person she'd once been. It seemed unwise to lose sight of one's former self, whether that self was good or bad or a little of both. The memory of it could be useful.

She closed her eyes and wriggled her body, snuggling further into the makeshift nest, letting the chirping of the crickets and the whispers of the light breeze toying with tree leaves lull her into repose.

The next morning, she woke, but only partially so, becoming vaguely aware of the sounds from the world around her awakening—birds twittering; the beeps, rumbles, and crunches of a garbage truck; the insistent barking of the neighbors' Pomeranian. She could hear them, but just barely. They seemed muffled, distant. And she couldn't see, or rather, when she peeked her eyes open, she saw nothing but light grey—almost white—surrounding her entirely.

Most days, she would have been alarmed by waking in such a state, but that morning, panic was the furthest thing from her mind. Despite the unfamiliarity of it all, she felt safe, warm, and billowy, swathed in down. In drowsy contentment, she sat, drifting in and out of sleep so seamlessly that she could scarcely distinguish dream from reality.

Sometime later—she had no good sense for how much—she began to hear voices, muted but perceptible and familiar. Her family members called her name and asked where she could have gone.

After a pause, she heard her name again, still muffled but louder. Then: "What's up in that tree?"

Soon after, she felt vague sensations of movement. The light grey of her surroundings flickered, like passing in and out of shadows on a sunny day with your eyes closed.

When stillness came again, she heard her father's voice. "Are you sure we shouldn't have left it be?"

"Of course," her mother said. "We need to protect it. To protect her."

"How can you be so sure?"

"A mother knows. Deep down, I think I've always known."

"But … how?" her father said.

From inside her encasement, Ava could not see their faces, but she pictured them: her father's dubious countenance and her mother's pensive consideration of his question. "I don't know," her mother said. "The universe is full of mysteries."

"Sure, but this? This isn't possible."

"Yet, here it is."

Ava smiled to herself. She'd worried about how her parents might react when the time came for her metamorphosis, but whenever she'd thought of broaching the subject, she found her tongue twisted in knots, unable to articulate words. Besides, what would she have said? How do you explain that your human body is only a placeholder? She hadn't known when or how the transformation would happen, only that it would.

Now that it was under way, her mother seemed to have at least some inkling of what was happening and sounded surprisingly calm.

"So," her father said, "what do we do now?

"We wait," said her mother.

"For how long?"

"That, I don't know."

Ava didn't know either, but it didn't matter much to her. She had waited all her life for this. She could wait a little longer.

She fell into a sort of suspended animation. Every so often, she woke, but never fully—instead, skirting along the fuzzy edges of consciousness as sounds of lawn mowers, laughing children, and car alarms from the outside world intermingled with her dreams. She didn't lose track of time—rather, she never had a firm grasp on it. Occasionally, she wondered how long she'd been inside her shell, hoping her parents weren't growing too anxious as they waited for her hibernation to end. Her mother would do her best to maintain an air of serenity all the while, but worry was bound to be lurking beneath the surface of her calm.

One day, she awoke fully, immediately feeling cramped and uncomfortable, unable to sit still for another moment. She began to move as much as she could, pressing on the walls of her encasement until they creaked and cracked. Then she pecked at the cracks until bits of shell fell away, letting in slivers of light and hints of cool air. She continued to peck, and finally, the shell split.

"It's happening," Ava heard her mother say as she wriggled and squeezed, extricating herself from the remains of the shell.

Free from her enclosure, she shimmied and shook, using all her muscles, familiarizing herself with the new configuration of her body. It felt odd yet so very right. Her vision was blurry, her eyes sensitive to the brightness of daylight after her time inside the shell. She blinked repeatedly, bringing her surroundings into focus, soon seeing with a depth and clarity she'd never known before. She stood atop a table on the covered porch. In addition to the hammock she'd used as her makeshift nest, a dog bed cradled the remains of her egg. She looked toward her parents—her mother beaming and her father gaping in awe.

"You're so beautiful," her mother said. "You've always been beautiful, but now ..." She left the sentence unfinished, but the unsaid words were plain. "Oh! You'll want to see!" She dashed into the house.

Her father looked her over, unblinking for longer than she would have guessed possible.

"I won't lie," he said softly. "This will take some getting used to, but I promise I'll try my best. I hope you can be patient as this old dog tries to learn some new tricks."

She bowed her head in a slow nod.

Her mother burst back through the door, carrying the mirror that lived on the entryway wall near the coat closet. She held it up.

Ava peered at her reflection, soaking it in. She was a bird—that was certain—but she was not quite like any bird she'd seen before. The feathers on her head were sleek and black, lending stark contrast to the orange-red of her beak. Below her neck, the plumage changed to dazzling greens down her back and vibrant shades of yellow at her breast. Her brilliant coloring resembled that of a songbird, but she was much larger, closer in size to a bird of prey. Truly unique. She vocalized for the first time in her new body, sounding a squawk of approval. Her voice was hoarse from disuse, and it came out quiet, so she squawked again, putting more force behind it.

Her mother's smile broadened, and she tilted her head. "How do you feel?"

Already, her new form was starting to feel like home. She raised her wings, tentatively at first, then lifted them higher, flapping them as she stood in place. Then she sprang into the air as if she'd been doing so all her life, flying out into a wide loop around the yard. How glorious! She could hardly wait to soar higher and longer, but she flew back toward the house. Her mother was awaiting a reply, even though she had probably already surmised the answer.

Some birds can speak, and Ava knew intuitively she was one of those. She alit back on the table where she'd hatched, folding her wings down and puffing up her chest. "I finally feel like me."

Fragments

Maureen tried not to panic as she struggled to piece together what had happened. Neither task was easy, as she had only shards of memories punctuated by disturbing blanks. The last thing she recalled was a frenzy of activity around her, almost hovering above her. Could that be right? She tried to grasp onto these wispy images and further examine them, but they were too vague. Even these faint inklings slipped away. The room was quiet now. She seemed to be alone.

With her memory failing her, she turned her focus to the present and what she might glean from her surroundings. She was on her back. This room was not a place she knew, but was not entirely unfamiliar either—a kind of generic space.

A flash of memory jolted her. Blue and red lights. A big white box. A voice…a man asking for her name. "Stay with me," he had said.

Again, she tried to get a firmer hold on the thoughts, but trying to do so only seemed to make them evaporate faster. She re-focused on the here and now. As nondescript as the room was, it must hold clues. The ceiling she was staring at revealed no answers, only square white tiles speckled with black dots of varying sizes. They were just like the tiles she recalled from her high school classrooms. Some days when the lectures had bored her, she'd counted those dots just to keep herself awake. Surely, she wasn't in her high school, though. This type of tile could be on any ceiling in any building in any room. There had to be other clues.

Until then, it hadn't even occurred to her to move, if only to sit up and look around, but as soon as she thought of doing so, she had a strange feeling, a tingling fear that she shouldn't. Not yet. It would be better to take in whatever else she could while remaining still. To her left was what appeared to be a monitor, but the screen was blank, void of information she desperately craved. Below that was a cabinet, or maybe a cart, with bottles, boxes, and some kind of tubing atop it. On the wall to her right was a phone, and mounted next to it was a trio of what looked like tissue boxes, but it wasn't tissue that peeked out from the openings. It was something not white, but vivid blue. Suddenly, the faint smell of latex struck her, and she understood the blue items to be gloves.

A hospital. That must be where she was. She spliced together her memory fragments into something approaching sensical—an ambulance, paramedics. These were bad signs, but panicking would do her no good, so she did her best to quell her fear. A quick mental scan of her body revealed no pain, which was somewhat reassuring. Of course, she might have been pumped full of drugs. That would explain the heavy fog lurking in her brain.

She heard a door open. At last, someone to help her fill in the blanks! The face of a woman, a nurse she surmised, entered her field of vision. Maureen attempted to speak but could not seem to get words to her lips. Still, she tried to keep her creeping panic at bay. Surely, the nurse would explain things. She just had to get her attention.

For a moment, she thought she'd caught her eye, but the nurse said nothing. Instead, she simply gazed down at Maureen. What was that look on her face? Sadness? Not exactly. Fatigue? A bit. But there was more to it than that. Whatever the look meant, it chilled Maureen through and through. Had it been so cold in the room the entire time?

Finally, Maureen tried to move, but her body made no response. Again, she attempted to speak, then to scream. Nothing happened. She looked desperately to the nurse, who responded only with a heavy sigh as she reached out her hand and gently closed Maureen's eyes.

The Game

Angela entered the world in the back of a cab, just minutes away from the hospital, clueless to the precedent she was setting. She couldn't recall when she started to recognize the pattern—it emerged gradually, in a self-fulfilling prophecy sort of way. But once she noticed it, she saw it more and more, in both present events and memories that she categorized retrospectively. Regardless of whether you believed there was some cosmic significance to it, once you saw the evidence stacked up, it was hard to deny: The most significant moments of Angela's life involved vehicles.

After the cab came the school bus where, at age six, she'd met Lacy, who was still her best friend 28 years later.

A family car was next. Her father sat behind the wheel with her mother riding shotgun. In the backseat, Angela and her sister Gwen vibrated with excitement as they neared the zoo. Tigers, monkeys, penguins, soft pretzels, and Bomb Pops paraded gleefully through Angela's mind, but the promenade ceased abruptly with screeching tires, a violent jolt, and a sound like a thunderclap. Sitting on the passenger side, farther from the impact, Angela and her mom had been relatively unscathed—not so for her dad and Gwen. Their family of four had become a family of two.

She'd met Josh on an airplane—perhaps the one time didn't mind being in the middle seat. Two years later, they were in a hot air balloon when Josh got down on one knee and pulled a black velvet ring box from his pocket. Some people said the balloon didn't count as a vehicle, but Angela couldn't see why it wouldn't.

On a Tuesday morning, Angela stood on a packed and stuffy train during her morning commute when waves of nausea began to pummel her. She took slow deep breaths, willing herself to make it to the next stop. When the train doors opened, she burst out and rushed toward a well-placed trash can, which caught what turned out to be her first bout of morning sickness. Months later, she was on a train again, this time headed home, when the cramps began. Light twinges at first, they intensified with disturbing rapidity, heralding that something was not right.

After the doctor appointment, Angela curled up on the couch, enveloping herself in the hand-knit throw from her late great aunt Hattie. Josh brought her tea and kissed the top of her head. "Maybe next time we need to conceive in a car," she said. Their red, puffy-eyed gazes met, and they traded the weakest of smiles at her attempt to dampen the pain with humor. But maybe there was something to it. Despite what the logical parts of her brain told her, it was hard to believe that all her milestone-vehicle connections were merely coincidental. It's not that she expected something life-changing every time she boarded a train or a bus—it's just usually where she was when the important stuff happened.

Back in college, Angela used to play a game: She'd pick a random number, get on the next bus or train that came along, and go that many stops. Her friends thought it was nuts, but the game had led her to find her favorite coffee shop and the animal shelter where she'd adopted her cat. Granted, she'd been mugged once while playing the game, but that could have happened anywhere. Besides, she'd been lucky—40 dollars and a cheap watch were all she'd lost. All in all, the game had brought her more good things than bad.

She hadn't played in years, and she desperately needed something good, or at least, something different.

"I'm worried about you," Josh had said. "I know you've been through a lot. It's been hard on me too. We can try again, but not in the state you're in."

The state you're in. Such vague words. Did he mean her grief? Her depression? Or was he intimating something more that he couldn't bring himself to say? What the fuck did he know anyway? Yes, the miscarriage had been hard on him, but he hadn't been the one with a person growing inside of him—a person who'd never be born, never take first steps, never go to prom, never eat a hot fudge sundae.

She'd decided to play the game again tonight, but as her workday wrapped up, a nervous apprehension squirmed in her brain. She chalked up to being out of practice, not to mention the ordeal she'd been through. A little something to calm her nerves, and she'd be fine.

Draining the last briny bits of her martini, she felt fortified, ready. All she had to do was get a number. The last digit of her bar tab was as good as any. Seven. Game on.

She texted Josh as she walked to the train stop. Still at work. Leftovers in fridge. Hopefully won't be super late. XOXO.

She hated to lie, but it was easier than explaining, especially via text.

A red line train rumbled into the station; its doors opened in invitation. Suddenly queasy, Angela sucked in a deep breath of the outside air before boarding. The martini had seemed like a good idea, but it wasn't playing well with the wine. There was a rhyme—wine before liquor, never sicker. Or was it beer before liquor? No matter—that ship had sailed. She sat down, shut her eyes, and breathed slowly while she counted the train stops. Seven seemed like a long ride, but it was better that way. Going only one or two stops would make it too easy to predict where she'd end up. She wasn't familiar enough with the red line route to immediately know where seven stops would land her.

At the seventh stop, she stepped out and stood on the platform. The cold air was a welcome respite from the overheated train car, reviving her, finally bringing her stomach to quietude. She looked out at the city skyline, the buildings gleaming with Lite-Brite majesty—such a big, beautiful place full of possibilities. So many potential destinations, but the game had brought her here. What would she find?

As she descended from the train platform, she spotted the church, standing out among all else, and felt a familiar pull. Something in her always knew where to go when she played the game. She walked toward the church. Was the universe telling her that religion was the answer to her problems? She'd never put much stock in it, but she was open to at least considering whatever the game brought her. It was the only way to play.

As she approached the church, she spied the sign out front and understood. Meeting at 7:00 tonight.

"Damn it," she muttered under her breath, glancing at her watch. It was 7:02. Close enough. She hurried up the pathway to the church door and pulled it open. The game didn't necessarily bring her where she wanted to be, but it did always seem to bring her where she should be.

Inside, she followed signs to the meeting room. The echo of her footsteps in the hallway sounded decisive, yet when she reached the door, she hesitated, hovering outside. "Am I too late?"

"Not at all," a 40ish man in wire-rimmed glasses said. "We were just about to do introductions for those who are joining us for the first time. You can start if you like."

Angela trembled. She could still make a run for it, but she steeled herself and walked into the room. She'd chosen to play the game, so she had to face what it brought her.

"Okay," Angela said. The bespectacled man stepped away from the podium and made a gesture to suggest that the floor was hers.

She stepped up to the podium and gripped its sides. A small sea of faces looked to her with expectant eyes. With an exhale, she felt her apprehension exiting her body, escaping out into the wide world. It had been a long time, but she knew what to do—what she had to do because, somehow, the game just knew.

She cleared her throat. "My name is Angela, and I'm an alcoholic."

I Shall Be Released

"Those were such strange times!" my parents often said. "You were a baby when the lockdown started. By the time things got back to normal, you were walking and talking."

Whenever they had talked about the early 2020s, I'd felt lucky to have no clear memories of those days. To me, the pandemic was just a collection of grim stories.

Everyone old enough to remember agreed: This new plague was much worse.

Trapped inside and stir-crazy, I consoled myself: It wouldn't last long—a few months at most. Drones delivered the necessities. Hologram calls eased my loneliness. Time marched on.

And on.

Along with the rest of the world, I pinned my hopes on a vaccine. One arrived, eventually, but with only forty percent efficacy, it did not set the world free.

My outlook changed so gradually that I hardly noticed the shift. Walls that once felt so confining became my weighted blanket: soothing and snug. Things I'd missed—restaurants, theaters, ballgames—seemed foreign; my memories of them, distant and abstract.

Then came the announcement: A definitive cure. Nanobots.

People burst from their homes, hugged each other with abandon. I watched from my window, longing to join them but finding myself unable. The idea of such things feeling safe was too slippery to grasp.

"It's time, Mom." Davian speaks firmly, but his face is placid and patient.

I shift my gaze away from the projected image of my son and gaze out the window. Davian and Jessie wave from the lawn.

I wave back feebly. "I'm scared."

"Just take it slow."

I try to pretend I'm simply collecting a delivery from my doorstep as I ease the door open. Warm air, faintly scented of lilacs, beckons.

With one diffident step, I'm outside. This might be all I can manage today, but it's progress.

Jessie beams. "Welcome back, Grandma!"

An Icing on the Cake

The last of the lights go out. I hear the click of the door being locked. Finally.

I stretch, slowly working the kinks out of my stiff joints. Standing still all day takes a toll.

Beside me, Nigel performs similar pandiculations. "I thought they'd never leave tonight."

"Seriously." I step down from the platform, kick off my shoes, and slump onto the royal icing surface of the display cake. I bend my legs inward and massage my feet with my hands.

Nigel smirks. "You always look so elegant in your gown, sprawled out like that."

"You try standing for hours in those things." I gesture toward the discarded heels. "See if you give a crap about looking elegant by the end of the day."

"At least you don't have a freakin' noose around your neck." He wrestles his bowtie loose.

I sigh. "We've all got our struggles." Our free time is limited. I don't want to spend it bickering.

An amicable quiet settles. Nigel removes his jacket, shoes, and cummerbund and undoes his shirt's top buttons. I slip out of my itchy tulle underskirt and release my skull from the tight, pinching headband of my veil, feeling the ache behind my ears evaporate instantly.

A scream shatters the silence.

"Mariana?" I whip my head around to see her bathed in the glow of a streetlight, her face squinched in horror. I follow the line of her pointing finger. "Oh, God!" Atop the center cake in the window display are Julia and Victor. They should be going through their after-hours routine—loosening up and getting comfy like everyone else. Instead, they stand stiff, lifeless, both without heads.

Shrieks and gasps reverberate through the shop as other toppers behold the grisly scene. Kaleb, Mariana's groom, springs into action, taking a running leap and landing on the middle tier of Julia and Victor's cake. Using the stiffened piping as hand- and footholds, he climbs to the top tier.

"Are they dead?" Mariana whimpers.

How could they not be? I don't know how Kaleb thinks he's going to help. Maybe he just needs to do something.

He scans his surroundings "Gah!" Looking down, he clamps a hand over his mouth and reels backward from the tier's edge.

I spot what Kaleb sees: Julia and Victor's heads, face down in a pink frosting rose on the cake's lowest tier.

"Who would do this?" Ida wails. She and her bride, Chelsea, cling to each other atop the leftmost cake in the window.

The question is met with only susurration, couples whispering amongst themselves. There's no lack of suspects. Julia and Victor were Lladrós—top-tier in every sense, inspiring abundant envy. But jealousy alone isn't proof.

I scramble to my feet. "Alright, everyone!" I try to sound authoritative, but the words come out screechy. I clear my throat. "There's a killer among us. I think we should all meet in the back office, on the desk, and figure this out." Back there, we can turn on some lights without drawing attention from outside. And if anyone objects to my plan: instant suspect!

There's a chorus of unintelligible murmurs, but everyone seems to be acquiescing, climbing down from their cakes.

Within ten minutes, we're all assembled beneath the glow of the desk lamp. I survey the group for any obvious clues. Their faces run the gamut: tearstained, pinched with worry, impassive.

"Who put you in charge?" Valencia says, hardly concealing her disdain.

"I don't claim to be in charge. I just thought someone needed to take the lead."

"Fishy if you ask me," she says. "Maybe you're the killer and want to steer suspicion away from you."

"Good question!" says Gabriel, Valencia's groom.

I shoot him a side-eye. "It wasn't a question." Gabriel's never struck me as overly bright.

He scoffs. "You know what I meant."

"Why would I kill Julia and Victor? I had no problem with them."

"Oh, like you didn't covet their window spot," Chelsea mutters.

"Well, if that's motive for murder, then everyone's a suspect," Mariana says. "Who didn't want that spot?"

Good old Mariana—always got my back. And she's right. "Exactly! Who wouldn't want to be front and center? But let's be honest—even with Julia and Victor gone, it was never going to be Nigel and me. We're nowhere near fancy enough."

Ida tilts her head, looking me over. "Good point. I mean, you're perfectly respectable toppers and all, but..."

I've never been more thankful to be run-of-the-mill.

"Valencia!" Mariana gasps. "She and Gabriel are the only other Lladrós on display. They'll probably get Victor and Julia's spot!"

All gazes turn toward Valencia. She grimaces, her eyes darting among our faces as she reaches into the folds of her gown to produce a sword—probably pilfered from one of the pirate figurines the shop keeps in stock for the occasional kid's cake. Brandishing it menacingly, she backs up toward a manila folder on the desktop. "Fine! I did it! I'm gonna be in that front window before this place closes down!"

"Closes down?" says Chelsea. "What do you mean?"

Valencia kicks the folder open and points to the document within. "I found this! It's a renovation work permit! They're going to gut Tiers of Joy—probably turn it into some awful chain restaurant!"

"No way!" Gabriel moves toward the folder and skims the document.

"Soon we'll all be tossed in the trash or boxed up indefinitely. Well, I'm going to have my goddam day in the sun first!"

Gabriel peels back the top document and examines the one underneath. "Um, Val?

"What?" she snaps.

"Says here they're upgrading the electrical so they can install new appliances. I don't think the shop's closing."

Valencia looks agape at Gabriel's discovery. While she's distracted, I lunge, grab her wrist, and wrench the sword from her hand.

I hold her at sword point, poised to strike if she makes any sudden moves. "What do you think, everyone? Maybe Valencia needs a ride in the mixer."

It Will Only Hurt for a Second

I've known from the beginning that that Julie isn't especially emotional. It didn't bother me at first. In fact, compared to my previous girlfriends, she was like a breath of fresh air. Before Julie, I'd dated more than my fair share of women who were…how should I put this? Erratic? Emotionally troubled? Like Cynthia—did I ever tell you about her? We dated for a while about a year before I met Julie. Things were great at first, but about two months in, she convinced herself that my working late was actually me cheating on her. Later, I found out she had her friends spy on me—not that they ever saw anything fishy because I wasn't cheating! But that didn't' matter because Cynthia had made up her mind. And she wanted revenge. She got my (former) best friend drunk and slept with him! But then I guess she felt guilty because told me all about it soon after, crying the whole time. I tried to break things off, but she went nuts and said she couldn't live without me. It was scary and pathetic at the same time. I just wanted her to stop crying, so, stupidly, I placated her and said we could try to work it out.

For maybe a month or so, things were better. She actually seemed sorry, like she realized how crazy she'd been acting. But before long, she started getting suspicious again. She practically interrogated me whenever I went somewhere without her. I wasn't cheating, but I started to wish I was. So, that time around, I didn't discourage her jealousy. If she was going to convince herself that I was messing around, I might as well let her believe it. Maybe she'd get fed up and dump me, save me the trouble. In retrospect, I guess it was kind of boneheaded. She could have just as easily gone bunny-boiling crazy. I was probably lucky that all she did was break up with me, even though I had to endure a screaming tirade in a coffee shop I haven't been back to since.

I'm sure you can see why I found Julie refreshing. She was so different, so even keeled. Not much fazed her. Hell, next to her, I looked like the overwrought one, which felt a little weird but kind of nice. Men are always expected to be the strong stoic ones for women to lean on. I must admit, it was nice to be able to do a little leaning for a change.

I don't want to make it seem like Julie was devoid of emotion. She was emotional enough to fall in love with me, even if her experience of "falling in love" was different from mine. She said yes when I proposed, so she obviously felt something like love. Anyhow, I knew how she was when I married her, so I can't exactly claim shock. I guess part of me thought that, while she was still single, she'd built up a wall to keep from getting hurt. I think a lot of people do that until they're sure a relationship is the real deal. I assumed the wall would break down after we got married. I just needed to be patient, and eventually Julie would show me her more tender side. When that didn't happen, I was surprised, even more so when it started to nag at me.

Again, feel like I'm painting an unfair picture. Julie wasn't completely cold. It's not like she flinched when I kissed her or shut down my sexual advances. Actually, she usually seemed to enjoy them quite a bit. She never initiated things, but I wrote that off as her being a little old-fashioned. When I told her I loved her, she usually said it back. Sometimes, instead, she'd just smile and kiss my nose, but that was kind of cute—like she was playing at being coy.

I told myself she loved me in her own way—there were lots of ways she showed it. She cooked, took care of the finances, gave me back rubs when I complained about being stiff, and brought me orange juice when I was sick. But it wasn't quite enough. A man can only say, "I love you," or, "You look lovely," so many times, give out so many kisses and embraces, before he wants some reciprocation. No—reciprocation isn't the right word. I wanted to feel like she wasn't simply parroting my I love yous and returning my kisses. Did I always have to be the initiator? Was a spontaneous kiss or I love you too much to ask?

I tried to lead by example. I doubled-down on my displays of affection—swept her into fervent kisses, told her she was stunning, even left her little love notes. I meant it all—I adored her, but I can't deny having ulterior motives. I hoped she'd realize I wanted to be treated the same way. But, well, Julie remained very much herself. It sounds ridiculous, right? Why should I have expected anything else? I still loved her, and I'd probably continue to love her even if things never changed, but this was really starting to bug me. The more I didn't get what I wanted, the more it bothered me, and the more I wanted it.

I tried to tell her how I felt. She was surprised—like it had never occurred to her that I might feel emotionally neglected. Still, she agreed that it wouldn't kill her to show me a little more affection. She said she'd try, and she put forth some effort for a few days, maybe a week, until she seemed to forget about it and things slipped back to the way they had been.

We went through this cycle a couple of times. Eventually, I got frustrated enough bring it up again. She apologized and said she'd try harder, but nothing ever changed for long. So, obviously, that wasn't working. I think Julie found the whole thing kind of silly—not that she ever would have told me that. Knowing she wasn't taking me seriously made me even more frustrated. She was the not-quite-normal one in this situation, not me! How could she not see that? And what's more, why couldn't she just give me what I wanted? Why did it have to be so damn difficult?

One raw day in March, the kind when winter and spring seem to be locked in a death match, I came home from work to find Julie sitting on the living room floor up against the couch. She was in tears, cradling Franklin's head in her lap, sniffling and gently petting his golden fur.

"Honey, what's wrong?" I said, dropping my bag and umbrella by the door. I hurried to her side, not bothering to take off my coat.

She looked up at me, her eyes red-rimmed and moist, and it struck me that this was the first time I'd ever seen her cry. I scanned my memory as I knelt next to her to offer whatever comfort I could. I had to be wrong. She had to have cried at some point in the eight years we'd known each other. My memory was able to drum up some images of somber looks on face, but her eyes were dry in all of them.

"It's Franklin," she said, interrupting the wild goose chase of my mind. "You know how his appetite has been off lately?"

I nodded and scratched Franklin behind the ears.

"I didn't think much of it. I knew he was due for some routine shots soon anyway, so I figured I'd mention it to the vet when I took him in for that." She paused and took a deep shaky breath. "This afternoon I got home to find he'd been throwing up—a lot—and there was blood."

I looked at Franklin. He seemed so content with his head in Julie's lap, like nothing in the world could possibly be wrong.

Julie wiped a tear away from the corner of her eye. "I took him to the vet, and they ran some tests… It's bad. They say he hasn't got very long—maybe a few weeks at most." Her voice cracked as more tears broke free from her eyes. I hate to imagine the look that must have been on my face. I wish I could say I had a concerned, sympathetic furrow between my brows, but it's more likely that I simply looked entranced. After all this time, I was seeing a new side of Julie. It was fascinating, even perversely delightful.

I put an arm around her, and she melted into my chest. "I'm sorry," she said between sobs. "I know this isn't like me."

Can you believe she was apologizing for showing me her emotions? "It's okay," I said softly as I stroked her hair. I felt a little excited as I said it and of course instantly hated myself for that. It's not like I wanted her to be in pain, but seeing her cry was such a relief. All was not lost! It almost made up for the bad news about Franklin.

Once she got over the initial blow, Julie was back to her usual self until about two weeks later when Franklin died. She cried again. I held her and cried along with her, partly for poor Franklin and partly out of self-loathing at my own happiness over seeing Julie's tears.

At that point, I think I managed to convince myself that things could be different. If Julie could cry for Franklin, surely she could be a little more affectionate with me. But nothing changed, except that I got more bitter. I mean, Franklin had been a good dog and all, but how could Julie muster more emotion for him than for me?

Weird, disturbing thoughts started popping up in my head. How would Julie react if I died or got some terminal illness? I told myself she'd be sad, devastated even, but deep down, I wasn't sure. Sometimes I pictured her standing beside my hospital bed or casket—stone-faced, unfazed—and panic swelled up in me. It's ridiculous—if I died, I wouldn't be around to see her reaction, so what was the point in obsessing about it? But damn, I wanted…I needed to know if she'd miss me.

The idea of a lame suicide "attempt" crossed my mind, but I scrapped it pretty quickly. It might have given me insight into how Julie really felt, but it also would have meant a bunch of questions about my mental health and endless prodding of my brain. Plus, there was the risk that my true motives would be discovered somehow. I was already afraid Julie thought of me as weak and needy, so I definitely didn't want that. But what then?

All this while, you and everyone else probably thought we were perfectly happy. Nobody knew what agony I was in. I needed to do something! One Saturday, I was ruminating on this, totally absorbed in my obsession, and I stumbled while walking down the stairs, missing a step but recovering my balance, narrowly avoiding a nasty spill. Then suddenly, it struck me—why not just fall? If I could do it without seriously hurting myself, I'd surely get some concern and sympathy from Julie. I'm sure it sounds insane, but I swear it wasn't just an impulse. I thought about it with a clear head. I made a rational decision. Then I closed my eyes, released my grip on the railing, and let my body drop. Let me tell you, this isn't as easy as it sounds. I had to fight off every instinct to catch myself, but I did it.

I won't lie. It hurt. A lot. My leg twisted beneath me, crunching grotesquely as I landed. I yelled and swore, and for a moment, I was sure I'd made a horrible mistake.

"What was that?" I heard Julie's voice before she reached the living room and spotted me on the floor. "Oh, God! What happened? Are you hurt?" She rushed toward me with concern all over her face.

I half-smiled, half-grimaced. "I think I may have broken something."

She looked at my leg and winced. Ankles were not supposed to bend like that. "We'd better get you to the ER.

Should I call an ambulance, or do you think you can make it to the car?"

"I think I can make it if you help."

I couldn't have dreamed of better results! Julie cooed with concern and positively doted on me while I was on the mend. I enjoyed the pampering, but that wasn't even the best of it. Finally, Julie's façade cracked. She seemed truly shaken when she speculated about how my fall might have been worse. "Thank God you didn't break your neck!" she said. At last, the confirmation I'd wanted! I could be sure she loved me.

Of course, broken ankles heal. By the time I was off crutches and in a walking cast, the old Julie was back—not cold, just reticent as ever. But since I'd had a taste of how things could be, I craved her affection even more. In a way, it was worse than before because I knew she had those feelings in her. Why wouldn't she let them out more often?

What could I do? The need for her affection gnawed at me. I didn't look forward to another injury, especially knowing it would have to top a broken ankle, but in the end, my desire won out. You remember my "accident" with the table saw? Yeah, not an accident. Oddly, it was easier than the fall down the stairs. It hurt less too. I had to psych myself up a bit first, but then it was just a matter of taking a deep breath and making one quick move. The table saw did the rest. Bam! Severed thumb! The blood spatter really added to the drama of the situation.

Despite that, the rush of attention I got from Julie was just barely enough to satisfy me this time. The doctors were able to reattach my thumb, and Julie's concern for me had regressed to the usual levels before the last of the bandages were off.

I needed another plan. I couldn't keep this up. The pain, not to mention the medical bills, would be too much, and Julie might start wondering why I was suddenly so accident-prone. I needed something bigger, not a mere physical injury but a deeper emotional scar. It had to be something that I could go back to again and again, for years even, whenever I needed some warmth—a hug, a kiss, a caress. Not just anything would do. It had to be big…a terrible, tragic loss… a death…the death of a dear friend, maybe?

So, now you know why I need to do this. I'm sorry it has to be this way, but I don't see any alternative. It really does pain me, but sometimes sacrifices are necessary. I know in the end it will be worth it. And as your friend, I promise you, it will only hurt for a second.

It's a Shame About Ray

My uncle Ray was dying. He'd been battling lymphoma for the better part of a year when Dad called to tell me that the latest round of chemo hadn't put him into remission and he'd decided to stop treatment. At most, he had a couple of weeks left.

"It would be nice if you could come up here to visit...before," Dad said. "I'm sure Ray would appreciate it."

Dad would never come right out and say that he was the one who wanted me there, but that didn't matter. I had to go. His little brother was dying. How could I not go?

But even as I told him I'd be there, I tried to think of some way to get out of it. I came up dry. I lived within driving distance—a long drive, but still, there was no excuse for not going. I felt bad for even trying to think of one.

My husband, Drew, was halfway across the country, which meant I had to do this alone. Drew rarely traveled for work, but a couple days earlier—of all times—his job had taken him to Seattle for a week and a half. "Just my luck," I muttered as I packed my overnight bag. As the words left my mouth, I wanted to take them back, snatch them out of the air, even though I was alone in the apartment. I was preparing to visit someone who was dying of lymphoma, and I was complaining about my luck. If I said that sort of thing when no one else was around to hear it, was I still a total heel?

"Are you okay?" Drew asked when I called to tell him about Ray. "Do you need me to come home?"

"No. It's fine." I really meant yes. Of course, I needed him. "It doesn't make sense for you to leave your conference." It didn't make sense for him to come home—except that I needed him to hold my hand while I did this. If nothing else, I needed a distraction. But Drew hardly even knew Ray, and I didn't want him to come home just for me. He would have if I'd asked him to, but I felt like that would have been venturing onto a slippery slope toward becoming one of those wives—pitiful and helpless without her husband. "I'll be OK," I said. "Stay in Seattle."

I sighed as I hung up. I was going alone.

Ray and I were what you might call acquaintance relatives. When I was a kid, we lived only about 25 miles apart, seeing each other regularly but not super frequently. Plus, at any family gathering, there were loads of people to catch up with: grandparents, multiple sets of aunts and uncles, and enough cousins that I sometimes got their names mixed up. Amidst all that, Ray and I never had conversations of much substance. How's school? How's work? Are the Brewers ever going to go all the way? That's about as far as we'd get. I hadn't seen him since my wedding—almost two years earlier. I'd be one of those obscure relatives coming out of the woodwork for a last visit. Would he appreciate it, or would it be too little, too late? Or worse, would it mainly serve to remind him that he was dying—as if he needed a reminder. Maybe he'd rather be surrounded by people he'd been close with all along.

But I said I'd go, so, I texted Dad to let him know I was leaving, and I headed north—alone in my car with little to divert my attention when darkness started to beckon at the doorway of my mind. As a rule, I avoided thinking about death as much as possible. Ruminating over it didn't make it any less inevitable, so what was the point? But sometimes, I found such thoughts inescapable, and before long, I'd feel smothered, pinned down under the crushing certainty that I and everyone I loved would one day cease to exist.

Podcasts weren't distracting enough. Stuff You Should Know faded to background noise as my mind followed the bleak path into gloom. Who would die first: Mom or Dad? Would I go first, or would Drew? Which would I prefer? What would my funeral be like?

I told my phone to stop playing the podcast and switch to music. Maybe some car singing would help me escape my thoughts.

I managed well enough for about five songs. Then I heard the opening chords of the old Lemonheads song, "It's a Shame About Ray." I hadn't heard it in at least a decade. What were the freaking odds?

I never really knew what the song was about. The stuff about putting the cobwebs back in place and Ray's name being engraved on a stone under the dust—it was all so vague and mysterious. I could bend the lyrics into whatever shape I chose. Usually, I imagined something shadowy and haunting—like the disappearance of someone I barely remembered but who still lurked in the far reaches of my mind. The song always gave me a sense of foreboding, which was amplified tenfold by the coincidence of it popping up just then. The universe seemed to be fucking with my head.

I could have prayed to God for a miracle to save Ray, but I'd long ago given up praying, given up hope that God was listening or there at all. Of course, if there was no God, that meant there was no one to be mad at. If God existed and had some master plan, there was someone to blame—someone to harangue about how unfair it was that Ray was dying, someone to ask what sort of sadistic master plan included this bullshit? Sometimes I wanted to believe in a supreme being so my anger would have a target instead of simply radiating from me, directionless and senseless.

Things like this shouldn't happen. Life should be fair. Ray shouldn't be dying. I wiped away the tears that had started to flow. Why was I crying over someone I wasn't even that close to? How would my life change after Ray was gone? I'd be sad, and for a while, he'd be heavy in my mind. I'd be forced to remember that life is precious and fleeting, that we have so little time—sometimes even less than we think. But all those thoughts would gradually fade, and I'd slide back into life as usual because you can't think about death all the time. It would start to eat holes in your heart.

So, aside from not seeing Ray at holidays anymore, my life would go on pretty much unchanged after he was gone. What was wrong with me? Shouldn't my uncle's death create a larger void in my life?

I arrived at the hospital parking lot and sat in my car, gearing up to go inside and fighting the urge to turn around and drive back to Chicago. No one would have to know that I'd come this far. I could tell Dad that I'd started to feel sick during the drive up and turned around, but as soon as the idea formed, I felt gross. He was dealing with enough. Lying to him on top of that would be super shitty. I got out of my car, took a deep breath, and walked toward the hospital entrance.

As I neared the end of the hallway where Ray's room was located, I spotted Dad sitting in a gray chair in the lounge area. "Hi, Dad."

He looked up from the book he was reading—always the real thing, no e-reader for him. "Hi," he said, rising to his feet and setting the book down.

I stepped closer and reached out to hug him. Dad isn't a big hugger. He's not averse to it, it's just not his go-to move. His hugs usually felt trepidatious, like he's not entirely sure how they work. But this one was different. His arms encircled me with the gentle pressure of a weighted blanket, drew me in, and held me there for several seconds.

"How's Ray doing?" I asked as we both withdrew from the hug. The words sounded wrong—too chatty to be asking about someone on his deathbed.

Dad sighed. He looked beyond tired, beyond sad. He looked depleted. "They have him as comfortable as possible. He sleeps most of the time, and when he's awake, he can't really talk—it's too much effort, but he can see and hear us."

"He can't even talk?" I'd had no idea lymphoma could take away your ability to speak.

"No, but he does respond a little. He'll move his hands and his eyes."

I nodded and looked down at the floor. Neither of us said anything for a few moments. There wasn't much left to do but go into Ray's room—the last thing I wanted to do. What if he died while I was there? I didn't know him well enough to merit being with him when he passed. I just wanted to remember him as he was the last time I saw him—smiling, happy, and having fun at my wedding. But I had to go in to see him. I couldn't very well show up, say hello to Dad, and leave. "Is he sleeping now, or can we go in to see him?" I asked.

"I'm not sure. He fell asleep a while ago, and I came out here to wait for you. We can go in and check, though."

Dad led the way. I stayed in the doorway until he looked back and motioned to me. I closed my eyes. Every cell in my body wanted to run back out to my car, but somehow, my feet carried me forward.

A month or so ago, Mom had emailed me a picture of Ray and one of his granddaughters who'd come for a visit. I saw the picture in my mind. Smiling, happy little Shelley with a stuffed cow in her hands, sitting at the bedside of her grandpa, who was a gaunt, hairless, shadowy-looking version of the man he once was. I wasn't ready to see that version of him in person, but I couldn't avoid it much longer.

When I opened my eyes, I trained them on the window, looking out at the dull gray tiers of the hospital parking structure, letting the image of Ray hover in my peripheral vision before looking straight at him. I blinked and slid my eyes over to the bed.

He looked much as he had in the photo—not good, but not like the image my mind had created of someone with so little time left. I wish I could say he looked peaceful. Maybe he looked as peaceful as possible for someone so skinny and bald, dressed in a hospital gown with an IV in his arm. But he was only 56. He'd fought a long, painful battle. He had five kids, eight grandkids, and a wife he was going to leave behind. There was nothing peaceful about any of that.

Ray's wife, Jenny, was dozing in the chair beside the bed. How long had she been there? Did she go home at night to sleep? Did she shower or change clothes? Can you even think about that sort of stuff when your husband is dying?

"Is he asleep?" I whispered to Dad.

Jenny stirred when I spoke. She rubbed the sleep out of her eyes and smiled at me sadly. "Lilah," she said, rising from the chair, "how sweet of you to come." She took one of my hands in both of hers and squeezed. By the haggard look of her, I wouldn't have guessed she'd have the strength to squeeze so hard. I fought off a grimace as my rings cut into my hands. I couldn't let her know she'd hurt me. Wasn't this poor woman going through enough?

"How are you holding up?" I asked, tilting my head to the side. Why did that gesture automatically accompany such a question? It was a ridiculous question anyway. No one wants the real answer: They're at they're not holding up at all. They've been crying their eyes out, cursing God, and torturing themselves thinking of all the things they should have said or done differently while there was still time. But you have to ask it. You're an insensitive lout if you don't. Besides, sometimes you just need to fill the murky silence.

"As good as can be expected," Jenny said with a slow nod.

Of course she'd say that. It was the only way not to lie without saying too much.

"And Ray?" I asked. Not that I didn't know.

Jenny sighed and looked over at her husband. "He sleeps most of the time now. It was such a hard decision…to stop treatment, but there wasn't much hope, and the chemo was so hard on him." She turned back to me. "He's made his peace with it, though. He's ready to go." Her voice was strained. She hadn't made her peace with it. She wasn't ready for him to go. And who could blame her? Who could be ready?

I thought of Drew. I could never be prepared for his death. He wasn't allowed to die—I needed to remember to tell him that. At least he wasn't allowed to die before I did. He'd handle my death better than I'd handle his. It's not that he wouldn't be sad, it's just that Drew handles everything better than I do.

"Well," said Jenny with a sigh, "I was going to go get some food, so I'll let you have a moment here. Can I bring you back a soda or anything?"

I shook my head. "Thanks, no."

Jenny left the room. I looked at Dad, at Ray, and back at Dad. What was I supposed to do now? I should probably say something. I should have prepared—at least had some idea.

"Do you want me to stay, or do you want a few minutes alone with him?" Dad asked.

"I don't know." God, I was clueless. "Alone…I guess. Is he sleeping?"

"I don't think so. I saw his eyes open for a second when we came in."

"OK," I said, looking back at Ray. How could someone in such a state strike so much fear into me? What was I afraid of anyway?

"I'll be right out in the lounge if you need me." Dad patted my shoulder and turned to go.

I opened my mouth to tell him to stay, but the words never came out and he walked out of the room. I didn't want to do this alone, but I didn't want anyone else listening either. If I said the wrong things, there would be no other witnesses—the words would die with Ray. I could even just stand there for a while and say nothing. Everyone would think I'd said my goodbyes, and no one would be the wiser—except I'd have to live the rest of my life with the thought that Ray died knowing that I'd come to see him and hadn't said a word.

Why were all my thoughts so horrible? Why did I keep making this about me?

I took a small step toward the bed. Had he fallen asleep again? Would it be wrong to wake him just so he could hear my awkward goodbye?

"Hi, Ray," I whispered. "It's Lilah, your niece." I cringed after I said it. Was I too loud? Too quiet? I didn't want to wake him, but at the same time, I did.

His eyes opened and then closed again. OK, he was listening.

I'd never had to say goodbye like this to anyone. I'd said goodbye to lots of people in my life, but never like this. Never to anyone I was sure I wouldn't be seeing again. Never a final goodbye.

I cleared my throat. "I don't know what to say. I…I wish all this wasn't happening to you. It's not fair." Great, Lilah, that's what he needs—tell him how much his situation sucks, as if he didn't already know. I shifted from foot to foot and struggled to find something to do with my hands, which suddenly seemed like they didn't belong to me. "I wish I could do something for you," I blurted out. "I wish I could make all of this disappear." It was true. At that moment, I felt like I would have done just about anything to make him not be sick. "But I know I can't. I guess what I want to say is that I'm sorry."

Finally, something I said felt right.

"I'm sorry I didn't come here before now. I'm sorry we never got to know each other very well and that I grew up so close to you but somehow so far away. I guess I thought there would always be time, or maybe I didn't think about it much at all." That was it, wasn't it? I hadn't thought about any of it until I'd been forced to. "I didn't come here to beg your forgiveness or anything, but I do want you to know that I'm sorry. I really am."

Ray's eyelids fluttered. I could barely see his eyes through the two tiny slits, but it was enough for me to know he was looking at me. A small smile crept across his face, and he gave me just the slightest little nod.

And with that, I understood why I was there.

I smiled back at Ray, and his eyelids eased shut. I reached for his hand, wrapped my fingers over his, and squeezed gently. Then I lingered for a few moments, silently holding his hand.

The Jumpers

Even on mild summer days, our apartment on the fourteenth floor of the high rise was stuffy. With the windows shut to retain the a/c-manufactured cool, the air inside felt overused, depleted of freshness. In the afternoon, sunlight streaming through the west windows could make you feel hot and cold at the same time. But that afternoon in July when the power went out, even after we'd pried open the windows, the apartment soon became stifling without even a fan to stir the air.

Early that evening, as the sun sank and the oppressive heat relented ever so slightly, my older brother Andy and I begged Mom to let us go outside, promising we wouldn't leave the block. It was still light out, and from our windows, we could see loads of people who'd ventured outside for some aeration and respite. We assured Mom we'd be fine—populated streets meant safety. Dark, deserted blocks were the dangerous ones.

Mom hesitated, raising an eyebrow and putting a hand on her hip. "You know no power means no elevator. If the power's not back on when you come in, you're walking up fourteen flights in this heat."

"We know!" we chimed. It would take more than that to dissuade us.

Mom exhaled and flicked her hand as if to shoo us out. "Fine. But you get back up here before dark."

We nodded our promise and ran for the door. In the hallway, we grinned at each other with our shared knowledge: forgiveness was easier to get than permission. Once daylight faded, the blackout would give us a rare opportunity for stargazing.

Outside, the temperature was still just shy of scorching, but it felt like a reprieve. The sun hid behind the buildings that jutted up from the lower jaw of the horizon like uneven teeth, and its slow but steady sinking promised more relief. Andy and I settled on a patch of grass near the northeast corner of our building.

Once the sun finally completed its descent, ushering in twilight, we could see a few stars right away. We lay on our backs, looking up, awaiting the arrival of their brethren—the ones normally drowned out by streetlights, shop signs, and the million other things that glowed all night in our neighborhood.

"Where do you think stars come from?" I said. I knew from science class that they came from gas and dust, collapsing under their own gravity over millions of years. But I didn't want the real answer. I wanted an Andy answer—a story.

I liked that he didn't blurt out the first thing he thought of. He took his time to come up with just the right thing to say. "They come from wishes. That whole wishing on a star thing is wrong. Stars don't make wishes come true. It's the wishes that create the stars. If a person wishes for something hard enough and long enough and if their intentions are pure, their wish will come true. And when it does, that makes a star. New stars are born all the time, but we can't see most of them because the universe is so huge and they're so far away."

I smiled up at the pinpricks of light. Andy's explanation was way more interesting than ancient clouds of gas and dust. Whose wishes had created Arcturus and Vega, and what had they wished for? Had any of my wishes ever created a star? I'd wished for a bike for my last birthday, and I'd gotten one, but I didn't think that was the kind of wish Andy was talking about. It had to be bigger, deeper, more important. Maybe someday, when I got older, I'd have wishes that were substantial enough to bring stars into being.

As the sky gradually darkened, I started to realize that I didn't really know how dark dark could get. City dark usually isn't all that dark, but the blackout changed that. Faint tingles started dancing along my spine. I wasn't scared of monsters coming out or anything silly like that. It would just be weird not to be able to see what's right next to me

But the power came on before the sky went completely black. People actually cheered. Hoots, hollers, and applause rang throughout the neighborhood.

The reillumination of streetlights, along with the lights from shops, houses, and apartments washed much of the luster from our stargazing plans, but Andy and I stayed put. The air conditioning would take time to catch up and transform our apartment into anything close to comfortable. With the sun gone and a slight breeze in the air, it was more pleasant outside than it was likely to be up there for a while.

As the last hints of twilight were fading from the sky, someone jumped. At first, I wasn't sure what I was seeing. A vaguely human shape suddenly appeared in the sky near the top floor of our building. I held my breath. Neither Andy nor I spoke.

Time slowed down as the jumper took flight. That's what it looked like at first—not falling but flying. I thought whoever it was might soar skyward away from the building instead of descending toward the earth. But maybe that was just me hoping amid the chaos and confusion that had suddenly penetrated my little life.

The jumper didn't ascend but instead lingered, suspended in the air like a cartoon character who hasn't realized they've stepped off the edge of a cliff. When gravity decided to operate again, it took its time, gently tugging, rather than yanking hard and sending the jumper plummeting straight down. The jumper drifted slowly earthward, fluttering this way and that like a leaf in the toying hands of a breeze.

For a moment, I thought maybe it wasn't a person at all. Maybe it was a dummy, a giant doll. It had to be. A real person wouldn't take so long to fall. But I wanted it to take even longer. I wanted to suspend time. I wanted the person, or whatever it was, to keep falling and never reach the ground.

The fluttering gradually dissipated, and the form's downward trajectory became more direct. Still, somehow, the longer it fell, the more space there seemed to be between it and the ground. Time stretched out like taffy.

What ran through the jumper's head? When their feet left the balcony, did they change their mind, regret their irreversible decision? Did they spend those moments in the air bracing for impact? Or were they too busy watching the movie of their life scroll by behind their eyes? Were their minds awash with happy memories? Teeming with regrets? Or were the images flashing through their heads bafflingly random? The Muppets lunchbox they'd had as a kid, its green thermos filled with tomato soup. The yellow monkey bar dome at the park near their childhood home, with the orange-brown halos of rust spreading out from each bolt. Their freshman year locker combination. The smell of sunscreen and the sweet fizzy goodness of orange soda on a hot day at the beach.

If I had time to think about all this as I watched, I could only imagine how drawn out the jumper's downward journey must have seemed. It reminded me of an old Twilight Zone episode. At the end, you find out that the entire episode was what ran through the mind of a man being executed by hanging. In those fractions of seconds between the time when his feet left the bridge and when the rope snapped his neck, an entire story plays out: The rope breaks, and he plunges into the river. He swims ashore, then runs for his life until he finally reaches his home. He and his wife are about to embrace when the scene cuts back to the man's body hanging from the bridge.

And that was just what could fit into a half-hour TV show (minus time for commercials). How much could time dilate in someone's mind between the moment when death becomes a certainty and the instant it actually takes them? The only people who learn the answer never have the chance to tell anyone. But maybe, in their minds, they live several lifetimes before it all ends. If I could think all this in the time it took the jumper to descend only a few stories, anything seemed possible.

I wanted to know what Andy thought about all this crazy stuff whizzing through my brain, but asking the question would have taken too long. Thoughts come so much faster than spoken words, and it seemed wrong to say anything. I don't know if I was being respectful to the jumper or if I was just afraid that I'd get distracted and miss something. Maybe a little of both.

A few floors up from where the first jumper had come, another form appeared. Then another from a couple floors down. Then two more from the other side of the building. I wanted to stand up and start yelling, tell everyone to stop, but I couldn't move, much less scream or even speak.

More bodies entered the air, so many that I lost count, and somehow, I knew there were just as many on the sides of the building I couldn't see.

The sky above was clear of clouds, but it was raining people.

But, like the first, the subsequent jumpers meandered in their descents—dancing, swaying, and twirling. I don't know how long we lay there watching this airborne ballet. It seemed like ages—so long that I almost forgot about the horror that would come when the jumpers began to reach the ground. But as they got closer, I couldn't seem to close my eyes or turn away. I was Alex in A Clockwork Orange, immobilized, eyes propped open. My parents had expressly forbidden me to see that movie, but I'd managed to anyway. I had nightmares afterward. What kind of nightmares would this scene spawn?

But then the strangest thing happened.

The first jumper neared the ground but never reached it. Instead of colliding with the earth, they sort of dissolved, morphing into a brilliant streak of light that twinkled as it faded like a horsetail firework. One by one, the other jumpers did the same, each turning to light and then fading away.

Andy nudged me and pointed. I followed the line of his finger, not toward any of the jumpers that were still aloft, but at the sky beyond them. We both lay there silently, gazing at the wide expanse above, watching new stars blink into existence.

Leave No Trace

Attention, time-cruisers: Please ensure you have all your belongings and only your belongings as you reboard. The recorded voice was pleasant but insistent. *Violators will be subject to fines and imprisonment. Items left in or taken from the past could lead to temporal anomalies.*

Stepping back onto the ship, Iona found herself mumbling along to the announcements she now knew by heart. They played on a loop whenever the ship was in port.

Cloaking devices must be used at all times while off-ship. Remember: Observe only. Leave no trace.

As pioneers in time travel tourism, Casimir Cruises made timeline preservation a top priority. It wasn't just lip service either. No one under the age of 18 was allowed, and would-be cruisers underwent psychological profiling to weed out those prone to fits of impulsivity.

Still vibrating with excitement from seeing Yo-Yo Ma not only alive but performing live, Iona hurried back to her stateroom, eager to gush about it to Vernon. They'd agreed to do their own things at this port. Thirty years of marriage had taught them that sometimes a little time apart was the best way to stick together.

Vernon looked up from his frenzied typing and smiled as Iona entered. "Hi, Sweetie!"

"Hi." She gaped at Vernon. "Please don't tell me you've been in here working this whole time!"

"Of course not!" He finished typing, stowed his tablet, and stood. "I got back a few minutes ago. I had some ideas I didn't want to forget."

"This is vacation, not a work trip."

"I swear, I just needed to get a couple things down." He encircled Iona in his arms. "I'm all yours now."

"I was only teasing." Iona kissed his cheek. She would never expect him not to make notes when inspiration struck. He was an inventor—mostly of toys and novelties. Sparks from virtually anything could ignite his creative passion. "Come up with anything good?"

Vernon's eyes glimmered. "New twists on some retro toys—I'll tell you over dinner. Speaking of…where should we eat tonight?"

"Hmm." Each of the ship's restaurants was themed for a historical period, with décor and cuisine to match. "Anywhere but mid-twentieth-century America."

Vernon opened his mouth, but the blaring of an alarm left his words unspoken. The stateroom went dark except for the flashing of red emergency lights.

Iona clutched at Vernon's arms. "What's happening?"

"The lights! It's a code."

Iona vaguely recalled codes being mentioned during orientation, but her mind felt scrambled by the clamorous siren.

"There!" Vernon lunged toward the stateroom door and scanned the placard posted there. "Red lights, flashing in threes…oh shit."

"What?"

"Catastrophic failure."

"What?!"

"Quick! The bathroom!" Grabbing Iona's wrist, Vernon pulled her into the tiny lavatory. He shut the door and pressed a series of buttons on the nearby keypad.

"Why are we in here?" The floor beneath them shifted, sending them reeling. Mercifully, the alarm ceased. The lighting normalized.

"Each stateroom's lavatory serves as a lifeboat. Remember? From orientation? In case of catastrophic ship failure, enter the lifeboat, disengage from the main ship, and wait for help."

How Vernon managed to recall all that under such extreme stress, she'd never know, but it was good one of them did. "What could have happened?"

"No idea."

The recorded announcement voice bubbled to the surface of Iona's mind. "Temporal anomalies!"

Vernon squinted and shook his head. "Nah…"

"It must be! They warned us a zillion times: Observe only. Even seemingly insignificant interactions with the past could upend everything."

Vernon's brows clenched into anxious furrows.

Iona's stomach dropped. She knew that look. "Vernon, what did you do?"

"Couldn't be…" Trembling, he reached into his pocket and pulled out his prized possession: the wind-up chattering teeth he'd had since childhood. Their red plastic was now marked with an illegible black scribble.

"What. Is. That?"

"I…I couldn't resist. It was once in a lifetime! It can't have caused this."

"What did you do?!"

Vernon slumped against the wall. "I had Eddy Goldfarb sign them."

"Who the hell is Eddy Goldfarb?"

"The inventor of Yakkity Yak teeth! And Kerplunk! And Milky the Cow! And about 800 other toys!"

Iona clenched her fists, exhaling her fury. "Do you mean that you may have caused temporal anomalies that led to catastrophic failure so you could get a toy autographed?"

Vernon's face quivered. "Sorry."

"Sorry?! Sorry that you might have destroyed life as we know it?!"

"That seems hyperbolic."

Iona threw up her hands and turned away. "Gah! I can't even look at you. What were you thinking?"

"We only spoke for a few seconds. He's a legend! I didn't think it would do any harm."

"FREAKING BUTTERFLY EFFECT, VERNON!"

"I'm sorry."

Iona softened at the gentle touch of his hand on her shoulder. "I guess we don't even know for sure what's going on. Whatever it is might not be your fault." She turned back toward him. "What now?"

"They'll send rescue ships."

"If there are any. Everything in our time could have changed."

The room lurched and shuddered with a crunching thud. The lights went dark.

"I think we landed," Vernon whispered. He groped along the wall for the emergency kit mounted there. A thin flashlight beam soon cut through the blackness, illuminating the kit's remaining contents. Vernon pressed the button on a small device marked Play me.

We at Casimir Cruises regret that rescue may be impossible in cases where temporal anomalies result in our nonexistence, said the familiar voice from the ship's announcements. Cyanide capsules have been provided for your convenience.

"Criminy," Iona muttered. "Where...when do you think we are?"

"One way to find out." Vernon pressed the Open Door button. Nothing happened. He yanked the handle, then yanked harder.

Iona joined his efforts. Finally, the door gave. A frigid blast and a wave of snow billowed in. From a few meters away, a wooly mammoth eyed them warily.

"Shit!" They slammed the door shut.

Iona shivered. In the inky cold, she heard a rapid clicking.

"Chilly out there," Vernon said grimly. He set his prized possession on the vanity and fixed the flashlight's beam on the teeth as they chattered.

Outside, the wind howled.

"We probably should have realized," Iona murmured. "People were bound to leave some trace."

Lifeblood

"Where's Jenna?"

Hearing the panic in Mom's voice, I wheel around and see the crowd reflected in her sunglasses as she searches.

"She was just here a second ago!" she says.

I scan the marketplace for my sister, attempting to be methodical, not frantic. "She can't have gone far." I try to keep my voice calm despite the alarms shrieking inside my head. She could have just wandered off, but I know in my gut that's not true.

Mom clutches my arm. "Milkmen?!" It's somewhere between a question and an anguished proclamation of what we both suspect.

I look toward the wharf and glimpse the kiwi-green ribbon in Jenna's long black hair as she disappears behind the corner of a gray brick building. I point. "There!"

"Go," Mom says, yanking the bag of produce from my hand. She knows she'd slow me down.

"Jenna!" I shout as I take off, zigzagging through the crowd as fast as I can.

I round the corner. The crowd is thinner here, but I don't see her. I tear off my sunglasses. It's overcast, so they only impede my vision. I'd only worn them to obscure the fact that I'm an

Immune. Jenna is wearing hers too, but the Milkmen must have identified her beforehand. They keep tabs on us—watching and waiting. None of us are completely safe, but I'm fast and strong, so I'm not the lowest-hanging fruit. Jenna fits that bill. She's small, even for her age. And if the Milkmen have been surveilling her, they know that she not only has Down syndrome but also wants to be everyone's friend. Vulnerable and amiable—a perfect target.

My eyes sweep the wharf. The Milkmen could have taken Jenna aboard a boat by now. And there are so damn many! I do the only thing I can think of—run down the nearest pier, calling her name, alert for any sign of her.

"Becca!"

I skid to a stop at the sound of my name and look toward the voice. Jenna grins and waves at me from a small boat that's pulling out of a slip on the next pier over. The Milkman raises a hand from the helm, flashing me a sinister grin as he waves too.

"Jenna!" I can't get to her. Fuck.

It's little consolation that Jenna isn't afraid. She should be. But, between her young age and the DS, she doesn't comprehend things like viruses and immunity. She wears the sunglasses because we tell her to. Someday she'll understand why we wear them: so we don't stand out as Immunes.

Once the virus gets into your nervous system, that's it. Barring the unlikely development of a miracle cure, you're dead within two years. Eyes are affected first, becoming so photosensitive that dark glasses are necessary on even the cloudiest days. From there, the course varies, but usually, brain centers involved in empathy and reasoning are next to deteriorate. So, it's not surprising a lot of people fall for claims that transfusions from Immunes can cure them. It's not true. Hell, if it were, I'd be first in line to donate blood.

But truth doesn't stop the Milkmen—scumbags who make bank by trafficking Immunes. Rumor has it there's a Milking

Station on an island about 40 miles offshore, where Immunes are kept sedated as their blood is routinely harvested for sale to the desperate Infected.

I sear the image of the boat into my brain and sprint back to the wharf. I keep one eye on the boat as I weave around people and press toward Pier 5. I'm so winded I can barely speak by the time I reach the jet ski rental kiosk where my friend Greg works. "Milkman got Jenna," I manage to sputter.

It's enough. "Shit." Greg springs to his feet, grabs a life vest and a key, and tosses both at me. "Sixteen!" he says, pointing the way

I nod thanks and bolt.

The jet ski starts on only the third try—small favors. I take off in pursuit of the boat. What the hell am I going to do when I get there? I'll think of something.

The Milkman turns and sees me approaching. I wish I was close enough to see the surprise that must be on his face.

Jenna spots me and waves. I can't help but smile as I throttle up.

I catch up with the boat and move into position along the starboard side. The Milkman jabs at me with a boat hook, which I manage to dodge as I wrap the dock line around the boat's railing. I kill the engine, and the sudden slowing of the jet ski, now tethered to the boat, causes the boat to lurch starboard. Thrown off balance, the Milkman stumbles headfirst into the railing. He groans, stunned and disoriented, but still conscious. I grab the end of the boat hook and pull it from his limp hand.

Jenna giggles at the Milkman. "Ouchy!"

"Jenna. Honey." My voice is firm but stolid. Jenna tends to freeze up when she's frightened. "Let's go for a ride on this. It's much faster and more fun than a boat."

Jenna tilts her head and looks from me to the Milkman, who's still sprawled out but starting to stir. She smiles and trots toward me.

The Milkman pushes himself up and reaches toward Jenna. "NO!" I scream as I squeeze my eyes shut and thrust the boat hook at his chest with everything I've got. I hear a thud and a sickening gurgling gasp.

I open my eyes and train them on Jenna, who stands motionless, gripping the starboard railing. "Look at me, Sweetie," I say, extending a hand. "We've got to go, OK?"

There's a glimmer of understanding on her face, and she gives me a small nod. She's scared, but she trusts me. Her tiny hand reaches for mine.

I close my fingers around it and hold on like I'll never let go.

Lullaby

She's too damn happy. That's my first clue. It's not that she's giddy or gushing—more that she has a newfound serenity, an amiability. Then, several days in a row, she wakes up with this low-key sly smile. That clinches it: she's cheating.

"Pleasant dreams?" I ask.

"Mm-hmm." She just keeps on smiling as if she doesn't notice the tinge of accusation in my voice or my smoldering glare.

I search her phone and computer. Nothing. I can't prove what she's up to—not yet. Her careful cunning makes the betrayal even worse.

I explain my predicament to Gus at I-Spy.

"I've got just the thing." He brandishes a device no bigger than a grain of rice. "This is some cutting-edge shit."

I'm impressed by its minuteness. "What is it?"

"A DreamCam. You put it behind someone's ear, and it senses the electrical impulses, the brain waves. Essentially, it records dreams. It sends the data to a computer, and you can watch someone's dreams like you're watching a movie."

It seems impossible—something out of science fiction. But Gus has always been straight with me, and if it works, it's exactly what I need. "How much?"

Gus strokes his beard in performative contemplation. "You're a loyal customer. I could probably knock a little off the price."

Even with the discount, it's more than I can reasonably afford, but it comes with a money-back guarantee. I take out my credit card.

I test it on myself first. Per the instructions, I pair the device to my computer, dab some adhesive onto the tiny rectangle, and press it behind my ear. If I hadn't put it there myself, I'd probably never notice it.

I lay awake that night, glowering at her in the dark, galled by her serene slumber. Even in sleep, she's smug. She's so damn sure of herself, so confident that I'm oblivious to her deception—she had no problem drifting off to dreamland, where, no doubt, she's enjoying another tryst.

Eventually, I fall into a fitful sleep.

When I first wake, I don't remember any specifics of my dreams, just faint impressions of old times, idyllic early days.

She leaves to go grocery shopping (so she says). I cue up the DreamCam footage. Initially, everything's hazy, disjointed the way dreams usually are. But then it's amazing, as if I've been transported back in time.

"I love you so much," I hear myself tell her. "I want to spend every minute with you."

She smiles. I feel the love radiating from her gaze. "You say the sweetest things. It just makes me melt." She rests her head on my chest and sighs. I can almost smell her shampoo and feel her warm, soft body nestled against mine.

This thing is worth every penny.

That night, I wait until she's asleep. To be sure, I nudge her and listen. Her breath remains slow and steady. She's out. She'll soon be dreaming of him—whoever the bastard is.

It's dark, but I can see well enough as I gently brush aside locks of her chestnut hair and put the DreamCam in place.

I slide back to my side of the bed and watch her for most of the night. Every languid shift of her body, each contented breath bayonets my heart as I picture what the camera must be recording.

At some point not long before dawn, I fall asleep.

It's late when I wake. The aroma of coffee mingling with something savory and faintly smoky draws me to the kitchen.

"I thought this might lure you out of bed," she says. She's standing at the stove, arranging a plate, adding finishing touches. A glass of orange juice waits at my usual seat at our breakfast nook. A vase with purple flowers sits off to the side. "Three-cheese and horseradish omelet with a side of bacon." She smiles and puts the plate down with a flourish.

Does she expect me to fall for all this?

I pick up the plate and the utensils bundled in the napkin beside it. "I need to check something for work." I turn to leave the kitchen.

"Don't forget coffee." She holds out a mug for me. Wisps of steam dance as they rise from the dark liquid inside.

I take the coffee and trudge down the hall.

I shut the office door behind me. The DreamCam is still on her, but she's within range. I upload the footage.

For several minutes, there's not much. I dig into my omelet as I watch a screen of gray static occasionally interrupted by flashes of images—random, mundane stuff: the calendar on the fridge, the vintage birdcage in the living room window, the wrought-iron fence encircling our yard, our garden in bloom.

Breakfast tastes a little off—not surprising considering how rarely she cooks—but it's passable, and I'm hungry. I'm almost done by the time something coherent begins to coalesce on screen.

Sunlight bathes our kitchen. She hums a dulcet melody—something familiar, although I can't immediately place it. Moving with a slow and easy grace, she picks up a brown bottle emblazoned with a comically large skull and crossbones and pours its inky contents into a crystal juice glass. "Da dee da da da da-do do-dum da," she sings, handing me the glass. Her voice is soft and saccharine.

I smile stupidly and drink.

"Da da da dum da-da-da do da dum."

I finally recognize the song, an old classic, redone time and again. My face contorts. I start to sputter.

"Dream a little dream of me," she sings, just above a whisper.

Through her eyes, I watch myself writhing in a badly acted death scene.

The image on the monitor fades. I shiver, although I'm sweating. My pulse quickens as the aftertaste of breakfast is replaced by a tingling numbness that spreads outward from my mouth. A burning nausea grips my gut.

Fuck.

I was right to be suspicious of her waking smiles.

Machinations and the Mystic

"Waste of money," Andy muttered.

The machine sucked my dollar into the slot, finally rewarding my diligent efforts to uncrumple it. Inside the glass chamber, Izabella's crystal ball began to shimmer and glow.

I rolled my eyes and elbowed my brother half-heartedly. "Mind your own beeswax." He didn't care how I spent my money. He just lived to razz me.

Izabella fixed her gaze on the luminous orb. "I see obstacles ahead." Her voice was rich and resonant, not the tinny crackle I'd expected from such a small speaker. "But perseverance will bring rewards."

Andy snorted. "How cheesy!"

"Is someone forcing you to be here?" I made a show of craning my neck, searching the arcade. "Go play Skee-Ball or something!"

"What? And miss Izabella's predictions?" His voice was soggy with sarcasm.

I knew the machine couldn't really foretell the future—I'm not an idiot. I thought it was fun anyway, but Andy just had to spoil it.

The machine whirred. A tiny paper scroll dropped into the drawer at the bottom. Andy snatched it up. I tried to grab it from him, but he held it up out of my reach as he unrolled it. "Let's see what the great Izabella has to say." He cleared his throat as if preparing to read aloud, then paused. His eyes widened as they scanned the paper. "Wha?"

I plucked the fortune from his hands.

When spent with enjoyment, time and money are never wasted. Also, mind your own beeswax, Andy!

Mettle Detector

Gemma smiled dreamily, watching billows of cream undulate in her coffee. It was a glorious morning, one that made her sure she was on the precipice of something wonderful—maybe a coffee shop meet-cute where she and some gorgeous stranger would simultaneously reach for the same stirrer.

As if on cue, someone sidled up next to her. "Listen carefully," the stranger whispered sideways. "You're in danger, but I'm here to help. Do what I say, and everything will be OK."

Gemma turned her head to see a girl—16, maybe 17—and chuckled. "Sure, kid. Whatev—" A shrill whizzing in her ear cut her off. The pitcher of cream on the condiment bar exploded, and a chorus of screams erupted.

The stranger grabbed her arm. Stunned, Gemma let herself be yanked out of the coffee shop. In one smooth, deft motion, the girl pulled something from her pocket and hurled it back through the door. Their assailant dropped to the floor amid the continuing cacophony of shrieks.

The girl pulled her toward a Vespa at the curb. "What's going on?" Gemma said.

"What's your name?" the stranger asked, mounting the scooter and starting the motor.

"Gemma."

"Gemma, I'm Tilly. Get on. I'll explain on the go."

"Go where? What's happening?"

"Listen, my throwing star bought us some time, but not much. If that guy doesn't come after us, there'll be others."

None of this made sense, but this Tilly, whoever she was, had saved her once already. Gemma clambered onto the scooter.

"Hang on."

Gemma gripped Tilly's sides as they sped off. Seconds later, a car screeched to a halt in front of them, blocking their path. "Fuck!" Tilly screamed, turning sharply, skidding them to a stop. She pulled a small, oblong item from the bag at her hip and appeared to bite it. Lobbing the object at the car, she spat something metallic from her mouth then gunned the scooter down an alley. The explosion behind them rattled Gemma's teeth.

"Was that a grenade?" Who was this girl? And why was she walking around with an arsenal?

"Yup." Tilly sounded almost nonchalant.

"What the hell, kid?"

"Hey, I know I look young, but I've been through more CDEs than I can count," Tilly shouted over the buzz of the scooter and the rush of air in their ears. "But I'm guessing you're new."

"New to what? And what's a CDE?"

"Character Development Exercise." They exited the alley onto a side street. "What do you remember from yesterday?"

It was an odd question against the backdrop of such craziness, but even odder was that Gemma had no memory of yesterday or much else. She had only a vague sense of her past, as though she'd skimmed a summary of her life. "Nothing."

"Yup, you must be a new character. The APA—All-Powerful Author—is coming at you with anything and everything. Seeing what you're made of." Tilly slowed the scooter as they turned onto a main road. "More traffic. Good. Maybe we can blend in. Hide in plain sight."

"Hide from who?"

"Not sure. Government operatives. Drug cartel hitmen. Evil cyborgs, maybe."

Gemma had so many questions, and everything from Tilly's mouth only bred more. "What do they want?"

"To challenge us. Test our mettle."

"Seems like they want to kill us!"

"Well, yeah. But what doesn't kill us reveals character."

Gemma wanted to scream. Or cry. Maybe both. Tilly wasn't making anything clearer.

"I know you're freaked," Tilly said, "but I think I've shown that I'm trustworthy. I'll do everything I can to get us over the bridge."

Gemma eyed the enormous suspension bridge looming ahead. How had she just now noticed it? Come to think of it, where were they? This place felt familiar but in a generic way—some nonspecific cityscape. "What's over the bridge?"

"Refuge—at least temporarily."

The ground rumbled as the asphalt beneath them cracked. Giant fissures opened in their wake. Tilly accelerated, swerving around cars to outrun a massive sinkhole that seemed to follow them, swallowing vehicles as it advanced.

"Lucky you're with me," Tilly continued, seemingly unfazed. "I'm the plucky teen who's way smarter and more capable than you'd think. The APA hasn't given me my own story yet, but I'm due."

A dull silvery object crashed to the earth in front of them. Gemma's stomach lurched as Tilly veered around what looked like a tentacled metal box.

"Kitchen sink!" Tilly scoffed. "APA's getting cheeky!"

Gemma read the sign as they crossed onto the bridge: Apogee River – Disbelief Bridge. Despite the chaos, things began to gel in her mind. "So, I'm a character? And all this is a writing exercise?" It made as much sense as anything else. She'd started the day in a rom-com mindset, but the APA clearly had other ideas.

"That's my guess. Hey, maybe you're my potential sidekick. Oh, shit!"

"What?"

Gemma followed Tilly's pointing finger to a small boat speeding toward the bridge. One of the men in it had a large gun trained on them.

"OK, would-be sidekick," Tilly said, "I need you to grab the gun from my bag."

"What? No! I hate guns!" Did she? She wasn't sure.

"Just do it!"

Gemma obeyed. The gun felt surprisingly natural in her hand. "Now what?"

"Shoot!"

She'd never shot a gun before, much less at a fast-moving target while she was also moving. But a barrage of bullets from below spurred her to action. She aimed the gun at the outboard motor, closed her eyes, and fired until the gun produced only empty clicks.

Opening her eyes, she saw a ball of flame where the boat had been.

"Nice!" Tilly shouted. "Right in the fuel tank!"

They cleared the bridge, and Tilly slowed the Vespa to a stop. Everything seemed sunnier on this side of the river.

Gemma shook her head "How the hell did I do that?"

"Sometimes, tropes are your best friends. Don't question it," Tilly said. A musical coda swelled around them. "Plus, I think the APA likes you."

The Night Watch

At first, they'd been merely a nuisance—strewing trash about the yard for Harlan to discover each morning. Not until the fencing disappeared did he begin to suspect they had bigger plans. They were plotting against him.

People called him paranoid, and even Harlan admitted it sounded crazy. That's why he was out here, crouching behind a gnarled oak with a night vision body cam clipped to his jacket. If it turned out they were just doing normal raccoon stuff, he'd drop the whole matter. But if he could prove they were up to more—well, that'd be something.

Rustling from the supposedly raccoon-proof trash bin alerted Harlan that one of the filthy buggers was in there, rummaging through the dreck with its creepy-ass hands, seeking edible tidbits and, if Harlan was right, other oddments—anything potentially useful for building, for weaponry. He'd stocked the trash with goodies as bait: old shingles, plastic sheeting scraps, hubcaps.

He waited.

Finally, the masked bandit scrambled out, clutching some bit of treasure in its mouth. It scurried off.

Harlan followed at a distance, keeping the rascal in sight, tailing it to the dilapidated old barn beyond his property line.

The raccoon scampered inside through a gap between the warped boards. Harlan stepped through the doorway.

As he reached for his flashlight, the toe of Harlan's boot caught something on the ground.

Snap. Clang.

Sweeping the light around him, Harlan gaped at the cage walls and the scores of glowing eyes admiring their catch.

The Nightly Grind

My uniform feels especially itchy tonight. I don't even understand why I have to wear it. Not being seen is part of my job! But some Fey muckety-muck decreed that Toothies wear tulle, so that's how it is.

I shouldn't gripe. Things could be worse. At least I'm not a Kobold, stuck underground, slowly developing black lung. Still…I wish I'd been born a Dryad. Protecting trees—now that's meaningful work, especially with the looming climate crisis.

I fly to my first assignment in a hoity-toity subdivision where kids get $20—for an incisor no less! If it were my money, I wouldn't pay half that, even for a canine. Plus, it's unfair that these bougie brats get so much while kids across town get only a quarter per tooth. Classist bullshit. But I don't make the rules.

"Opna," I intone. The lock clicks, and I ease the door open. Inside, I see the flashing light of an alarm system. Dammit, that wasn't on the spec sheet!

"Afvopna," I say. The light keeps flashing. Alarms—what a pain. I never know which spell will work.

"Leysa."

Nope.

"Dekryptere…Avkoda."

The light flashes faster.

"Fokk," I mutter as I type 1234 on the keypad. The flashing stops. I exhale with relief and roll my eyes—brilliant passcode.

I flit up to Quentin's room, grab the tooth, and leave the cash under the pillow.

I can't help myself. "Omorganisere," I whisper on my way out. I smile, imagining the family's bewilderment at finding their kitchen drawers rearranged.

Not a Morning Person

The sound is familiar. Music—rhythmic synth pangs, then a galvanic drumbeat and a voice you recognize: Beyoncé. But that doesn't make sense.

Not once did you question how you came to be in this tropical paradise—somewhere you don't need sunscreen at noon in July and the air temperature is always perfect—or why the water is the color of orange popsicles for that matter. Never mind that—it's the music that baffles you. Your canoe rocks as you look around, trying to discern where the sound is coming from, scanning the banks as if you could have missed Beyoncé and a brigade of backup dancers busting their moves riverside.

Then, suddenly, you're no longer in the canoe.

Your mind is fuzzy. The source of the music is still a mystery, and now you're also wondering what happened to the flamingo. He'd been regaling you with a triumphant story from his college football days, but he abruptly vanished just as Queen B began to proclaim that girls run the world.

Your thoughts seem slow, like they are swimming through honey, but mere seconds elapse as you realize the flamingo was part of a dream, which you immediately forget. Later, when you see the pink flamingoes on your shower curtain, the name

Arvid will pop into your head, but you won't know why. You won't remember the story about his Rose Bowl–winning touchdown.

But that's later.

Reality seeps into your brain bit by bit. You identify the source of the music: your alarm. You're in bed. You can't discern what day it is, but your heart swells with the hope that it's Saturday and you've set your alarm by mistake. The image of a W drifts into your mind, followed by eight more letters. Wednesday flickers on your mental marquee. Your hope is squelched.

What do you usually do on Wednesdays? Go to work. Unthinkable as it seems, you sense it's true.

You half-heartedly attempt to open your eyes, but your eyelids resist. How unreasonable of you to request something so drastic!

Tiny impulses that never make it to your conscious mind address your eyelids: "I don't like it any more than you do, but, seriously, you've got to open."

The eyelids relent, opening to the thinnest of slits. The one consolation to waking so early is that the room is dim. Reassured by this, your eyelids ascend to half-mast.

You turn your head toward the source of the sound: your phone in its dock on the bedside table. Your still-sluggish eyes can't make out the numbers on the screen. You blink and squint. Blurred digits come into focus, but they're meaningless—a random arrangement of squiggles. You blink again and decipher their meaning: 6:00 AM.

Your mind gropes for excuses not to leave the bed. You could call in sick. Actually, how do you feel? Maybe you are sick—it's so hard to tell at this hour. You could quit your job and move somewhere tropical. Maybe there was an overnight snowstorm and you won't be able to get to work—no wait, it's May. But this is Chicago, so there's always a chance.

More signals from your central nervous system call your right hand to attention and assign it a mission. The hand complies begrudgingly and crawls out from under the covers. It pauses, suspended in the air as messages are relayed back and forth from hand to brain. Reports from the expedition confirm what had been suspected: It's too early, and you're too tired—so tired, in fact, that the hand struggles to maintain its position. It musters its remaining energy to swat at the orange oval on the screen marked snooze then retreats to the safety of the blankets.

Not Tonight

I'd had one of those days that just drained the life out of me. I fell into bed, thankful that sleep would soon provide a brief escape from my life of drudgery. As I lay there, just beginning to drift off, I felt Ben inching towards me. He wrapped one arm around me and started to kiss my neck. I could have pretended to be asleep, but if I did, he'd probably just try to wake me up anyway. "Please honey, not tonight. I'm dead tired."

He didn't stop. "I'm sure you can stay up a little while," he whispered as his tongue flicked my ear.

"No, seriously. It's been a long day, and I'm exhausted." He probably thought I was saying it just to avoid having sex. He always took it so personally, but I was just tired--the kind of tired where it hurts to keep your eyes open.

"Please." His hands began to reach up under my nightgown.

"No," I said softly. "Tomorrow night. I promise."

"God, sorry." He pulled his hands away. "I'm sorry making love to me is such a chore."

"It's not like that." How did he always do this? How did he always turn me into the bad guy?

"Come on," he said, moving closer to me and touching me again. "Can't you do this for me?"

"I told you. I'm tired."

"You don't have to do anything," he told me. "You can just lay there."

I don't know how that was supposed to entice me, but that's essentially what our sex life had become--a series of lackluster encounters that he guilted me into. I had no energy for passion anymore, but I didn't have the energy to fend him off either. He would wear me down and make me feel like the worst girlfriend in the world if I said no.

"Please," he said again, already tugging at my panties.

"Okay," I said and hated myself for giving in. I was just reinforcing the idea that if he whined and begged enough, I would give him what he wanted. I stared up at the ceiling as he went to work, his fingers and his mouth exploring me. A lump grew in my throat, and I tried to swallow it. Crying would only make things worse. I should quit feeling sorry for myself. I'd given in, but it wasn't as if he was raping me. If I really wanted him to stop, he would. Probably.

I winced as he entered me, and I bit my lip to stifle a sob. Tears began to roll down my face. Did he realize? Did he care? If anything, he would probably make me feel guilty for crying and making him feel bad. Maybe I deserved this humiliation for not being strong enough to stand up to him.

My body tensed. It wouldn't be long now. That was the one consolation. He never lasted all that long. How pathetic--that was the best thing I could say about having sex with him.

When he was done, he kissed my tear-streaked face. "Thank you," he said. "I love you." He rolled over and fell asleep almost immediately. I stared at him, watching his body slowly move up and down with each breath. I picked up my pillow. If I could just smother him with it, he would never humiliate me like that again. Instead, I threw the pillow back on the bed and went into the bathroom where I could cry in private so I wouldn't wake him.

Pith and Pretense

Leila feigned interest in the nearest sculpture as she moved behind it, glancing quickly over each shoulder to make sure there was no one in back of her—all clear. With the artwork as cover, she wriggled her hips, reached underneath the skirt of her sky-blue charmeuse gown, and tugged on the legs of her shapewear shorts. They had ridden up into a torturously uncomfortable position. That'd teach her to buy knockoff Spanx.

She sighed, relieved of her discomfort. With that off her mind, she regarded the sculpture in front of her. Was sculpture even the right word? Installation? Heck, she should just call it what it was: A pile of avocados.

It's not that Leila didn't enjoy contemporary art. She just preferred her art to be more…accessible. But this? Leila circled the pedestal beneath the heap of green-black produce, searching for its label—Seeking Salutations. This kind of stuff she did not get. It seemed pretentious and purposefully abstruse. Worse, it was a waste of perfectly good avocados! Plus, knowing how quickly they went from rock hard to complete mush, she wouldn't be surprised if Avocado Swapper constituted a full-time position at the museum.

No matter. Tonight was really about raising money for the Sickle Cell Alliance. The venue was bait to lure in donors. This evening's gala provided an exclusive after-hours preview of a much-touted exhibit that wouldn't open to the public for another week, along with the chance to meet some of the artists—although exactly which ones was a well-guarded secret. Leila had been heavily involved in planning the event, and not even she knew. But she'd never heard of most of the contributing artists anyway. The important thing was that turnout was great, and the Alliance was on track to meet its fundraising goal. For that, she'd gladly smile and nod as attendees discussed the Deep Meaning of stacked avocados or the Pivotal Nuances between two completely white five-by-five canvasses. Leila found them indistinguishable, but she was willing to fake rapt attention for anyone whose formalwear had deep pockets.

A tuxedoed server extended a tray toward Leila. "Thank you," she said and took one of the flutes filled with effervescent straw-colored liquid. Once the server had moved away, her lips curled into a sad smile as she lifted the glass and silently toasted Aaron. He'd been gone almost two years now.

A lot of her friends told her it was time—past time even—to get on with her life. And by that, they meant finding someone new. What people didn't seem to realize is that she had gotten on with her life. Her work with the Alliance was a way to honor Aaron's memory, but it was so much more than that. It gave her a sense of purpose and fulfillment like she'd never had before. She hadn't found someone new, but she'd found something new, and she was happy, for the most part. Sure, she got lonely sometimes, and if someone new happened to come along, she was open to that. She just couldn't see herself chasing after romance, though. She had better ways to spend her time and energy.

She sipped her champagne and noticed a nearby group of patrons gathered in a semicircle around something. Curious, she sauntered over to see what they were looking at.

"It's certainly eye-catching," said a woman Leila could only think to describe as a middle-aged goth. Her iridescent blue-black corseted gown wasn't something Leila ever would have worn, but she had to give the woman props—she was totally pulling it off. "But I don't know," the woman continued, "it's so violent!"

Leila shifted her gaze from the woman to the artwork that had attracted the group's attention. A single green olive sat on a small white plate. A red pimento drooped, partially extruded, from one end, and a clear cocktail pick that pierced the fruit's flesh stuck out at an oblique angle.

Leila sipped her drink again as she stifled a laugh. A strikingly handsome man sidled up beside her to join the semicircle. His close-fitting charcoal-grey suit hugged a Men's Health–worthy physique. He gave Leila the faintest of smiles and a nod of greeting. Leila returned the nod and felt her face get hot while a fluttering sensation arose in her chest.

"Violence is the point!" said another man who Leila had already sized up as an art student with a trust fund. "The olive represents an eye—the constant surveillance we're under as we're tracked, both online and in the real world. The pick signifies rebellion—skewering those who perpetrate these invasions of privacy."

Several members of the group began to nod slowly as they digested the statement. It sounded like grandiose nonsense to Leila.

Mr. Handsome shook his head. "I don't buy that at all."

Here we go, Leila thought, bracing herself for the battle of grandiloquent rhetoric that was sure to follow—one of the more genteel displays of toxic masculinity that wealthy men seemed to favor.

"Is that so?" said Trust Fund, straightening his spine.

Handsome smirked. "It is."

"I'd love to hear your interpretation." Trust Fund didn't try to hide his goading.

"It's not interpretation so much as intent," said Handsome, "seeing as I'm the artist."

Trust Fund's face fell amid murmurs and at least one gasp from the semicircle. He tried to mask his embarrassment by hastily donning a smarmy grin. "Please, then, enlighten us!"

Handsome smiled, shrugged, and tilted his head. "I'm just not a fan of olives."

As if on cue, a busser swooped in and cleared away the "artwork" the group had been admiring. The semicircle members—except Leila and Handsome—muttered and scoffed as they dispersed, slinking away in chagrin.

Leila laughed and looked at Handsome, whose smile was now directed toward her. "I didn't lie," he said. "That was my plate."

There was that fluttering in her chest again. Leila became aware of something, long dormant inside her, stirring awake.

Recompense

The pain of the first penetrating stabs tears through me, sharp and searing. Still, I struggle against you, flailing and clawing, believing I might be able to escape. Then the knife punctures my lung, and I feel it collapsing—not the quick pop of a balloon, but a slow, pathetic deflation. Do I hear a hissing gurgle as the air slithers out, carrying with it my hopes of survival? Or am I imagining that?

As my life drains away, I feel a merciful reprieve, but only from the physical pain. In my last living moments, our eyes meet, and where I expect rage, instead I see perverse euphoria. With your sickening smile, you deal me one final, lasting torment. It's little solace to realize how passionately you once must have loved me if you could grow to despise me so thoroughly.

Afterward, I hover, never leaving your orbit, watching, waiting, hoping for justice. But you are clever and charming, your cleanup meticulous. You expunge every stain, leave no clues to be found. My case grows cold. You live on. As if nothing had happened. As if I'd never mattered.

Decades pass. Time is something I will never want for again, but it is closing in on you. Coughs rattle your tumor-riddled body. That's only the beginning, the first of many payments you'll make, not just for the life you took from me, but for every moment you've enjoyed since.

Can you hear the hounds? They're coming. Snarling and hungry.

I'll stay just long enough to watch them drag you away. Then I'll find peace.

Regarding Emma

As a parent to be, you hope your child will be perfect. Of course, you know she won't be, but that's okay. She'll cry and keep you awake half the night. She'll spill things on the rug. She'll lie and talk back, and she'll rebel against you when she's a teenager, no matter if you're a permissive parent or if you run your house like a military unit. John and I expected all of that normal kid's stuff. We thought we were going into parenthood with our eyes open. It wouldn't always be a picnic, but we would weather the hard times because the good times would make it all worthwhile. Our child wouldn't be perfect, but she would be ours, and we would love her.

My pregnancy was trying, to say the least. For one thing, my "morning sickness" wasn't confined to the morning. I was sick more often than I wasn't, but that was just the tip of the iceberg. I developed a terrible rash on my stomach. It itched and burned so much that there were times when I wanted to claw through my belly. At first, the doctors thought it was some kind of heat rash, but the usual remedies did nothing, and the rash didn't subside when the weather turned cooler. My doctors were stumped. The rash didn't change, didn't spread. "Some women have unusual reactions to pregnancy," they shrugged and said to me.

Once the baby started kicking, she rarely stopped. I could hardly get a moment of rest as she twitched and flailed within me. "Oh, she's an active one, isn't she?" Dr. Morgan, my ob/gyn, noted during one of my checkups when Emma seemed to be trying to kick her way out of my womb.

"Yes. It never stops," I said.

Dr. Morgan chuckled. She thought I was exaggerating. "I know it can certainly seem that way sometimes, can't it?" she said.

"No, I'm serious. She never stops." But right then, as if to prove me wrong, the baby stopped kicking. I came off as the nutty, hormonal, anxious first-timer who thought her pregnancy was worse than anyone else's in history.

All tests suggested that nothing was medically wrong with Emma. She would be a perfectly healthy, normal baby. Things would be fine if I could just get through the remainder of those awful nine months.

Alas, the misery didn't end with the pregnancy. From just about the minute Emma was born, it was clear that she was different. When the nurse drained her mouth just after she entered the world, Emma began to scream. It wasn't the typical newborn baby cry. It was an ear-piercing, bone-chilling shriek, like she was being torn apart. And then just as suddenly, she was totally silent. The doctor and nurses exchanged nervous glances. Physically, Emma seemed fine, but everyone in that room knew something was wrong.

John was at my side when the nurse handed Emma to me and I held her for the first time. I had waited so long for that moment. After more than a year of trying and then nine months of torturous pregnancy, I was finally going to hold my precious little girl! Perhaps I'd built up such high expectations for the moment that nothing ever could have lived up to them, but when I held Emma for the first time, it wasn't just that I didn't feel the rush of total elation I had expected. I actually felt my heart fall. I had heard some women say that they wished the moment they first held their child could have lasted forever, but I wanted it to be over as soon as it had started. What the hell was wrong with me? Could this be some weird side effect of the pain meds? Was it too early for postpartum depression? Was I just an awful, cold person who was unfit to have a child?

I told myself that I was probably just freaking out about being someone's mother. After all, my life was never going to be the same. But still, I was sure it would be better. I just needed to calm down and take things one step at a time.

I held Emma for a few minutes, hoping the whole time that it would start to feel right. It didn't. My face must have given me away. "Honey, are you all right?" said John.

I forced a smile. "I'm fine. I'm just exhausted." That had to be the problem. I'd feel normal again once I'd had some rest. "Do you want to hold her for a bit?"

John gingerly lifted Emma from my arms. As he held her, I watched his face slowly change from surprise and confusion to concern and then to panic. It wasn't just me. Our eyes met, and we silently asked each other the same questions. "What is wrong with our little girl? What is wrong with us?"

That first day was only the beginning. Emma spent most of her infancy alternating between shrieking and eerie silence. I tried to breast feed her, but I physically could not do it. It was as if my milk shrank away in horror. In a way, I was relieved. I hated myself for it, but the thought of several months of nursing Emma actually made me nauseous.

John and I both got used to holding Emma in the same way you get used to a dull chronic pain. Whenever a friend asked to hold her, we quickly handed her over, grateful for the reprieve. No matter who held her, the reaction was always the same. A look of shock was followed by the sudden remembrance of a pressing task that needed to be done or the abrupt development of a scratchy throat or some other ailment that the baby shouldn't be exposed to. Emma was then handed back hastily. Eventually, people just stopped asking to hold her. No one ever spoke ill of Emma to our faces, though. You just don't tell new parents that holding their daughter makes your blood run cold. At least we could take solace in the fact that it wasn't just us.

When she was an infant, Emma couldn't do too much harm, and it was a little easier to dismiss the feeling that something was wrong with her. But the older she got, the harder it was to ignore that she was not like other kids.

Kids wreck their toys. They usually don't mean to, but sometimes playthings just aren't built to last. So, I expected broken toys here and there. I hadn't expected 15 decapitated dolls and stuffed animals, but when I walked into Emma's room one day when she was six years old, that was what I found. The heads were lined up in a neat little row on Emma's bed, and the bodies were in a jumbled pile in the corner.

"What's this, Emma?" I asked, as calmly as I could. I had gotten pretty good at disguising my horror.

"It's my collection."

I knew they were only dolls, but what the heck kind of sick kid tears the heads off of her toys and makes a collection out of them? Was I overreacting, or was this another sign that my daughter really was a monster? "But honey, why don't you just keep a collection of whole dolls? Why just the heads?" I asked.

Emma seemed confused by the question. "I like tearing them apart." She said matter-of-factly, as if the answer should have been obvious to me.

Perhaps I should have pressed her further and tried to figure out why she liked destroying her dolls, but I must admit that I was afraid of what else I might discover, and I didn't think I could stand to be more afraid of my own daughter than I already was.

John and I originally planned to have at least two kids, but once Emma was born, we knew we couldn't handle another child like her. Even if our second child was normal and totally unlike Emma, we were more than a little afraid of what kind of horrors Emma might inflict on him or her. John got a vasectomy.

Please don't think that I just gave up on Emma without trying. I took her to more counselors than I could count. As awful as she was, she was also brilliant. She deceived all the doctors and therapists by telling them what they wanted to hear. I'm pretty sure that, deep down, every one of them knew something was wrong with Emma. I think everyone who met Emma got that feeling, but she said all the right things, and no doctor is going to tell parents that their daughter is simply creepy.

We had tried Emma on about half the drugs on the market by the time she was eight years. Eventually, she decided she was done with all of that. "I am not taking these anymore," she calmly told me one morning when I set a glass of juice and her dose of Ritalin on the table in front of her.

"Come on now. It's for your own good." Even as I said it, I knew it probably didn't matter. Just like all the other medications, the Ritalin didn't seem to be doing any good.

She picked up the juice, but instead of drinking it and taking her pill, she threw the glass at my face. It hit me in the mouth, cutting my lip. As I stood there, bleeding and dripping with orange juice, Emma gave me a hollow, cold stare of someone who just might kill me if only she were a little bigger and stronger.

Not surprisingly, Emma had real no friends, but that didn't seem to bother her. It was of constant concern to her teachers, but oddly enough, Emma didn't get into serious trouble at school. I think that was merely because Emma was too smart to get caught. There were incidents. Katie Wilson was rushed to the emergency room after eating a cookie that had crystal drain cleaner mixed in with the sprinkles on top. When she was asked where she got the cookie, Katie said that it had just been in her lunch box. Her parents were investigated but eventually cleared.

Old Mary Perkins down the street came over with flyers one day. Her cat had gone missing. "He must have seen a critter or something that got him awfully excited because it looks like he clawed right through the window screen!" About a week later, Mary went to the basement to get some ice cream and found her cat in the freezer.

I think everyone, including John and me, believed Emma was to blame for all of these things and more, but no one had any proof. Emma denied any involvement, and I left it at that. I know I was in denial, but who would want to believe that her daughter could do such horrible things?

If only I had been braver, maybe I could have helped her or at least convinced a doctor that she needed to be locked up where she couldn't do anyone harm. But people don't just lock kids away without hard evidence that they've done something pretty awful. Now you have that evidence. John and I will live the rest of our days with the knowledge that we didn't do enough and three people are dead because of it. If I could turn back the clock and do something, anything, that would have prevented all this, I would. Of course, I can't do that, and that is why I am urging you, the jury, to give Emma the maximum sentence for her crimes. I beg of you, lock her up and never let her out.

Requiem

Something isn't right.

I can't recall when it started, but somehow, I know I've been slow to admit it, brushing the feeling aside until it could no longer be ignored. The not recalling is the problem—or at least the main symptom. Things keep slipping through the grasp of my mind. Events that should become memories, if only short-term ones, flow through like water through splayed fingers, leaving only dampness as evidence that they were there—just enough for me to sense that something is missing.

Have I always been this way? Maybe this is normal for me. Shouldn't I know that? I feel like I used to be different, but that could be wishful thinking. If I haven't always been like this, perhaps I can get back to the way I once was.

As if emerging from a dreamless sleep, often, I find myself in strange places. Or rather, the places aren't so strange as my not knowing how I got there or why I came. I should probably find this alarming, but for some reason, I don't. Where distress should be, there is only curiosity. My lack of alarm should trigger its own disquiet, but, of course, it doesn't.

During my mind's nimbler moments, I think this must be dementia. Again, I'm not alarmed, just a little sad, mainly for my family and friends. To me, the forgetting, the flitting in and out of lucidity, and the lack of resulting distress are kind of lovely, but they must be hell on my kith and kin.

Family. Friends. I assume I have these. I feel that I must, although their names, their faces escape me.

Sometimes, images come to me in odd flashes: memories, I think. But remembering them catches me off-guard. How can they be memories if I can't recall ever remembering them before?

One of them hits me now—practically bowls me over—a new memory from long ago: A sort of game we used to play as kids. When you're passing a cemetery, you have to hold your breath until you're past it, otherwise, you'll die.

I inhale deeply and hold in my breath as I walk among headstones and floral bouquets in various stages of wilt, hunting for clues. Why have I come here? Likely, to visit someone's grave. But whose? Am I mourning the loss of a cherished someone? Perhaps this is another blessing of dementia: adeptness at drawing a veil over my own grief.

I scan gravestones—the ornate, the plain, the weathered, and the pristine—searching for a name to spark another memory, remind me why I'm here. Part of me doesn't want to know, but it feels important. I should figure this out. It could be the key to unraveling this mystery of how my mind has gone awry, why I forget things even as they are happening to me.

My gaze comes to rest on one of the newer headstones, its polished granite still glossy and unblemished. The date to the right of the dash is mere weeks ago. The name carved into the stone stirs something within me, rings a faint but familiar bell. The monument denotes that the decedent was a beloved wife, daughter, sister, and friend. I knew this person—I'm certain of it—yet I cannot conjure a mental picture of her. I feel it in my bones that we were close, but memories of her are sequestered somewhere deep inside me, inaccessible. I try to remember, but I don't try too hard. Remembering would make me sad.

It's better this way.

Before long, I'll forget that I couldn't remember. Maybe I'll be distracted by another foreign yet familiar recollection as it rises to the surface in my swamp of a mind.

I turn and walk on, past the headstone.

I realize I'm holding my breath. Why? Has my mind decayed so much that I've forgotten to breathe?

No matter. There was a time when I needed to breathe. But that time is past

Śavāsana

I'm a bundle of jagged nerves. I'd already been keyed up from dealing with lawyers, plus continual angry texts and voicemails from Theo, my soon-to-be ex-husband. Then, my car started making a noise that I know will cost me at least five hundred dollars to fix. On top of that, I need to rejigger the class schedule because of Chelsea's upcoming maternity leave. This will mean weeks of calls and emails from perturbed (and frankly, rather entitled) yogis who'll feign courtesy while lamenting the chaos and blocked chakras that these schedule changes have triggered.

I get to my studio early, intending to start the day with nice long meditation so I can be as grounded and centered as possible in the face of the shitstorm that currently is my life.

I set my bag on the window bench and put the lights on their lowest setting. Something's off—it's too dark. Looking up, I see that one of the bulbs is out. My exhale is half sigh and half whine. Aren't LEDs supposed to last practically forever? I trudge to the back closet, grab a fresh bulb and the stepladder, and return to make the swap.

When that's done, I light a stick of my favorite jasmine incense. The warm scent is a balm for my frayed spirit. I turn on the soundbar, and the room soon fills with the susurration of ocean waves. Already, I'm feeling lighter, more serene as I unfurl my mat and position myself in śavāsana.

"Perrin? Are you OK?"

The voice draws me back to consciousness. It's Naomi, who teaches the noon vinyasa class. Damn. Not only did I fall asleep, but if she's here, apparently, I slept for hours.

I sit up slowly, blinking the sleep away. "I guess I dozed off. I was meditating and—"

"Perrin?" Naomi takes a trepidatious step toward me, her eyebrows knit together with concern.

"I'm fine. I just—"

"Perrin?" Naomi leans down, extending a hand to give my shoulder a gentle shake.

That's when I notice my shoulder isn't where it should be. I scramble to my feet, trying to understand what I'm seeing: my body, still lying on the mat, still in śavāsana—corpse pose.

I back away as a flurry of activity begins around my body. Naomi attempts CPR. Paramedics arrive. I watch my body lurch from the jolt of the defibrillator, but I feel none of it. The cops come next. The scene unfolds before me like a film on fast-forward. Nothing makes sense.

Unless I'm dead.

But that doesn't make sense. I'm only 31. I'm the healthiest person I know. I own a yoga studio for God's sake! I can't be dead.

I need to focus. I muster all the concentration I can, and the world slows, gradually returning to normal. I move forward again, inching back toward my body.

"Let's get these ceiling fans going." The woman—Detective Sanders if I'd heard correctly—looks at Naomi. "Any chance that opens?" She points to the front window adorned with the studio logo: a lotus flower encircled by the words Moore Shanti.

Naomi, whose face is streaked with tears, shakes her head as she switches on the fans. "No, but I can prop open the door."

"Good," says Sanders. "Whatever killed her has probably dissipated by now, but we should increase ventilation as a precaution."

Diego, the other detective, tilts his head. "What are you thinking?" I get the feeling he has ideas but wants to hear his partner's thoughts first.

"My gut says this wasn't accidental."

Sanders' words are a kick in the teeth that I didn't see coming. But does anyone expect to be murdered?

"No signs of trauma, though. The only thing weird is her skin."

I follow Diego's eyes. With the studio lighting now at its brightest, I can see that my skin is practically glowing, a cherry-pink hue.

"Carbon monoxide?" Diego offers.

"Could be." Sanders looks doubtful. "But from what? The furnace isn't on this time of year."

"Water heater?" Diego says. He looks to Naomi.

"In the basement," she says. "It's electric, though."

Diego frowns. "Maybe some other environmental toxin?"

"The ME should be able to tell us more," Sanders says, but as she scans the room, I sense she wants to figure it out first. She's searching for confirmation of something she intuitively knows. Her eyes home in on the table against the wall, which holds a trio of bronze yoga pose figurines, along with my ceramic incense plate. She strides over and leans in for a closer look at the small heap of ash collected atop the mandala design on the plate. "Incense could be the culprit."

"I'll bag it." Diego dons blue gloves. He puts the plate and the remnants of the incense into a bag marked Evidence.

I loved that incense holder. It had been one of Theo's more thoughtful gifts, back when things were good.

"Is burning incense an everyday thing here?" Sanders asks.

Naomi sniffles. "No. Perrin liked to, but some of our regulars complained because it aggravated their allergies. So, we don't use it during classes anymore. Sometimes Perrin would burn some when she was here alone, though."

"Could be a tainted batch," Diego says.

"Or someone who knew the vic's habits tampered with it," Sanders says with a slow waggle of her head. She looks again toward Naomi. "Can you think of anyone who might want to hurt Ms. Moore?"

"God, no! Everyone loved Perrin." She pauses. The shock on her face gives way to disquiet.

"What?" Sanders says.

"She's going through a divorce."

Sanders and Diego exchange knowing glances.

"But no. Theo would never…" Naomi shakes her head, but doubt tinges her voice.

No. Theo wouldn't hurt me. Not my husband…the chemist.

I don't know whether I'll stick around here or move on to some other plane. But while I'm still here, the first thing I need to do is figure out how to haunt that bastard.

School's Out

This is the last time, Allison thought as she approached the ugly brick building. Finally, four years that had felt more like decades were coming to an end today, her last day of high school. As she made her way into the school and through the hallways, it was impossible not to notice the nostalgia swirling around her. People exchanged yearbooks, undoubtedly scribbling solemn promises to be friends forever. No one approached Allison, which was fine. She wasn't the slightest bit sentimental about Jefferson High. She wouldn't be cherishing memories from her years here.

At her locker, she spun the dial to enter the combination her fingers knew by heart. Once again, her eyes passed over the remnants of the word cunt that had been scrawled on her locker door in permanent marker and mostly, but not completely, removed by a janitorial staff member. She'd never known who'd written it—the suspect pool was too large to focus on any one person of interest.

Allison told herself she didn't care, but that was BS. It's not that the word hurt her exactly—infuriated was more like it. Maybe...probably she was a cunt, but it's not like any of her classmates would know. They hadn't bothered to get to know her. Granted, her demeanor hadn't really invited that, but at the very least, her fellow students could have simply left her alone. Even if she had no friends, not being actively bothered by anyone would have made her high school years infinitely more tolerable. But no. They couldn't let her be.

She'd tried to shrug it all off, telling herself that people wanted a reaction, and if she didn't give them one, they'd eventually get bored and move on, finding an arbitrary reason to designate someone else as pariah number one. But there was only so much she could take before she'd crack, and eventually, she'd lash out. That was enough to keep her tormentors going.

Ever since she'd started to formulate her plan, she'd gotten better at ignoring the taunts and teasing. Whenever she felt ready to explode with rage, she closed her eyes, breathed deeply, and pictured the day she would show them all. That day had finally arrived, but as she shut her locker and headed to her first-period class, she puzzled at her lack of emotion. Mere hours away from executing her plan, she'd expected herself to be giddy with anticipation—nervous but exhilarated. Instead she felt flat, empty. Maybe she'd built it up too much. All along, she'd told herself it would change everything, but there had been a nagging suspicion in some dusty corner of her mind that was now scratching its way to the forefront—what if it doesn't change anything? Sure, people probably would be shocked and sad for a while…then what? Would they sweep it out of their minds and continue as if nothing had happened? What's more, how would Allison even know what impact she'd had?

Time crawled during her morning classes. Textbooks were collected, evaluation forms were completed, and free time was given for yearbook signing. Allison doodled in her notebook through most of it, all the while trying to make sense of the flat feeling inside her where once there'd been such relish. Maybe all the joy had been in the planning—imagining everyone's reaction. But when it came down to it, hanging herself on the stage of the commons during lunch might not actually do a damn bit of good. It would definitely be dramatic—for days she'd spent time before and after school figuring out how to rig up a system that would pull open the curtains as she rocked the chair from beneath her. But she wouldn't be able to revel in the drama, no more than she already had in her head anyway. So...what was the point?

High school had been hell, but dead or alive, she'd be leaving it behind soon. Was she just losing her nerve and trying to rationalize chickening out? Maybe. But then again, perhaps it's true what they said...that living well is the best revenge.

The lunch bell rang, and students shuffled out of classrooms. Allison's heart began to pound. She swam along with the sea of people at first, but when the crowd continued straight toward the commons, she darted left toward an emergency side exit. As she opened the door, an alarm sounded. She stepped outside, felt the sun hit her face, and broke into a run.

The Sign

"Just give me a sign that I'm doing the right thing." I say it under my breath. Who am I talking to anyway? I feel sort of stupid asking, but I guess I'm just looking for some reassurance that I'm making the right choice. After all, having a baby isn't something to take lightly, especially at my age. And of course, people's opinions on the matter are always biased, so I'm putting the question out there to the universe.

I've been over and over it again in my head, and I'm pretty sure I've considered everything. It's not as if I can be completely rational and objective this it, but I like to think I've come as close as possible. This is what I want. This is what makes sense for me, but here I am, second guessing myself and asking for a sign that it's the right thing to do. Does that mean that part of me is looking for a way out? They say you're never one hundred percent certain about big decisions like this, but I just want to be as sure as I can be.

I shiver and cinch my coat tighter around me. It's effing cold out for September, but I can't take that as my sign because it was already effing cold out when I asked for one. If I don't get a sign before I reach the clinic, I'll keep walking, and donor number 841's sample will just have to wait. It's not as if I couldn't do this on another day. I haven't got forever, of course, but I do have some time. The clinic employees are probably used to rescheduling. I'm sure people lose their nerve all the time.

Maybe what really matters here is my reaction to whether or not I get a sign. I draw closer and closer to the clinic, and I don't see anything that I would consider a sign. What is it I'm feeling. Disappointment? Nervousness? It's so hard to tell. Am I rooting for a sign? I think I am.

I know that I don't actually need a sign in order to do this, but I also know myself well enough to realize that, now that I've asked for a sign, I'll have to wait until I get one. And the more time that passes, the less sure I'll be of what I should consider to a sign. It would be so easy to spot a sign as I take these last few steps to the clinic, but it doesn't look like one is going to appear.

I pause in front of the clinic door and look up at the sky. "Well?" I say, as I close my eyes for a moment and give the universe one last chance. I feel flakes of snow fall onto my face, and I smile.

Suckers!

Kayla tried to quell her trembling as she stood at the tree house window, balancing a bulbous green water balloon on the business end of a spatula. From below, a peal of raucous laughter heralded the boys' approach.

"They're coming!" Amy whispered.

Kayla placed the fingertips of her free hand on the spatula's edge, just like Laurie had shown her. Beads of sweat dotted her forehead as she waited, poised to fire. She swallowed hard. Three boys came into view, loping along like oafs. With a flick of her wrist, she snapped the spatula up and forward, launching the balloon. It sailed in an arc through the thick summer air and landed squarely on Randy Boyd's head with a splat.

Laurie and Amy erupted into laughter.

"Nice shot!" said Laurie.

Kayla ducked down below the window and felt her muscles untwine as she sat on the floor and started to laugh along with the other girls. She was officially in the club now.

A few minutes later, Randy was still wet but hot with anger, pacing in his back yard. Kyle and Adam sat nearby on the porch steps, barely suppressing their laughter, further stoking Randy's fury.

"I'm so sick of them! We need to retaliate!" Kyle and Adam probably didn't even know what retaliate meant. Maybe the big word would wipe the smiles off their stupid faces and remind them why he was the group leader, albeit unofficially.

"What are we gonna do?" Kyle asked.

Randy stopped pacing and narrowed his eyes. "We're gonna steal their candy stash."

The boys' eyes widened. The tree house candy stockpile was the stuff of neighborhood legend.

Dusk settled, painting the sky with streaky clouds in grapefruit and tangerine. Adam peered through his binoculars, which were trained on the tree house. "They're leaving!" he announced.

"Are you sure?" said Kyle.

"Course I'm sure, dummy. They're climbing down the ladder right now."

Randy grinned. "Excellent. Gentlemen, it's almost time. Everyone remember their jobs?"

Kyle rolled his eyes. "Yeah," he muttered.

"What's your problem?" Randy demanded. A less benevolent leader wouldn't abide such insolence.

"I don't wanna be the lookout. It's no fun."

Randy stifled the urge to tell Kyle to shut up and do what he was told. He knew a gentler approach would yield better results. "It's an important job!" He clapped a palm on Kyle's shoulder. "A good lookout could make or break the operation. And you'll get an equal cut of the candy."

Kyle didn't seem convinced but at least looked less dejected. "Oh, all right." He picked up the broom that lay on the ground beside him.

Randy looked at him expectantly.

"I stand watch, and if I see someone coming or any sign of trouble, I signal by swiping at the windchimes with the broom."

"Good." Randy nodded. "Adam?"

"I've got the note." From a pocket of his backpack, Adam pulled a sheet of notebook paper. Large block letters in red marker looked menacing on the page. He read aloud, "Revenge is sweet, and you're all suckers! The Boyd Brigade."

"Are you sure you wanna say Boyd Brigade?" asked Kyle. "They'll know it was us... or at least you... who took their candy."

Kyle was just jealous. Randy was the leader, so it made sense that the group should have his name. Besides, Boyd Brigade sounded a heck of a lot better than Sanders Squad or Thomas Troop. Kyle's and Adam's names just weren't as good. "We want them to know who took the candy," Randy said. "It'll teach them not to mess with us."

Kyle nodded and shrugged simultaneously.

Randy smiled but clenched his teeth. If Kyle didn't quit being so oppugnant, he might end up with a smaller share of candy. "Okay, as Kyle keeps lookout, Adam and I go up. The candy stash is probably hidden, so I'll search the west side of the tree house, and Adam, you search the east." Randy punctuated his speech with gestures to his right and then his left.

"East is that way," Adam said, nodding his head in the direction opposite to where Randy was pointing.

Randy's nostrils flared. "I said west. I go east. Adam, you go west!" Geez, Adam clearly wasn't listening. His candy share might have to be cut too.

"Huh," Kyle chuckled. "Adam West." Randy and Adam looked at him blankly. "You know... the old Batman?"

"Can we focus here?" Randy hissed.

"Sorry," Kyle muttered and turned his eyes toward the ground.

"Whoever finds the candy puts it in their backpack. We don't know how much there is, so if it doesn't all fit, we'll split it between our packs. Then we get out of there quick-like and meet behind my garage. Got it?"

"Got it!" Adam and Kyle said in unison.

As the last wisps of daylight vanished and the buzz of cicadas dwindled to silence, the boys set off on their mission, creeping into Laurie's back yard. Kyle held his broom at the ready and crouched to make himself inconspicuous while Randy and Adam bolted toward the tree. Randy grasped the rope sides of the ladder and began to climb with Adam close behind.

When he reached the top, Randy sneered at the "Keep Out!" sign on the trapdoor entrance, pushed the hatch open, and hauled himself up into the tree house. He flicked on his headlamp and started to sweep the room with its spotlight. Up against one wall, a large pink tackle box sat atop a whitewashed wooden table. "That's gotta be it!" Randy said as Adam came up through the door and turned on his headlamp.

"Easy peasy!" Adam smiled and pulled the note from his backpack.

The boys stepped toward the box. Randy licked his lips, released the front latch, and flung open the lid. There was a click, then a pop. As windchimes jangled in the distance, the boys' headlamps illuminated the spectacular explosion of glitter that engulfed them.

Three Minutes

Click.

Okay, so now I wait. Three minutes. Three long minutes. And then…what? I guess I'll jump off that bridge when I come to it. Maybe I won't have to do anything at all. I could be worrying for nothing, but five days is pretty late. I'm usually like clockwork. Oh God, please don't let the stick be blue. It can't be blue. It won't be blue. I was careful. I made sure he wore a condom every time. Lots of people do it with no protection at all. Are they sitting here listening to the sickening tick-tick of a timer as they wait for their entire future to be revealed to them by a stupid stick? I'm the one doing that, and I used protection every single time. How freakin' unfair is that?

God, what will Kurt say? He won't want me to keep it. I can just picture his face. Will he even try to hide his fright and try to comfort me at all? I don't even know. Jesus, I don't even really know my boyfriend, and I might be carrying his child!

Never mind Kurt, I don't even know if I'd want to keep it. How could I? But how could I not? This is impossible.

I won't have to decide because the stick is not going to be blue. Right? Right. Positive thinking!

I hate the commercials for these tests. They all have happy couples with the wide smiles. Where are the people like me?

We're the ones buying the tests, but I guess people pacing and wringing their hands, chanting, "No blue, no blue," wouldn't make the best ad. It really doesn't matter. The ad people could put Hannibal Lector in the commercials and we'd still buy the tests. When you need a pregnancy test, you need a pregnancy test, no matter what's in the stupid commercials for them.

Please, please, please, don't let it turn blue!

Fifteen year-olds have babies all the time. How the hell do they do it? I've got six years on them, and I'm sitting here thinking about how my life will be completely turned upside-down if the damn stick turns blue. Am I really less equipped to deal with this than a fifteen year-old? What is wrong with me? I'm not a kid. I'm twenty-one! God, wasn't I just fifteen yesterday? My life is still just beginning! Oh, God, just give me a few more years. I just started my job four months ago. How are people going to react to my taking maternity leave? A young, unwed mother—how did I become this?

Relax. Deep breaths. I'm not a mother yet. I still a minute and a half left in limbo.

What if Kurt wants to do the so-called honorable thing and marry me? I don't even know if I love him. I've only known him for six months. How could I marry him? And if we did get married and have a kid, we'd have to move to the suburbs and buy a minivan, and then I may as well just lie down and wait for death. I hate minivans. I hate the suburbs. God, I'm going to get fat too. Then Kurt won't even want me anymore, and he'll run off with some bimbo and leave me to sob uncontrollably and start drinking vodka in the middle of the day.

Damn it. Why didn't I go on the pill? I'm such an idiot for putting off going to the doctor for so long to get a prescription. What the heck kind of mother will I make if I can't even manage to that?

Okay, just calm down. It won't be much longer now. This stick is not going to be blue. Everything will be fine.

How can I possibly support a child? I have student loans and obscene credit card bills. I can't afford a baby! Diapers, clothes, food—and I don't want to think about how much daycare costs. I'm going to have to stay home and take care of the kid because I can't afford daycare. Then I'll have to go on welfare, but I still won't be able to afford my rent, so I'll get evicted and will have to live on the street and beg for change.

No. No. No! None of that will happen because the stick is not going to be blue. There are plenty of reasons I could be late. Work has been crazy lately, and didn't I read somewhere that stress can make your period late?

How can three minutes last so long? This seems like ten times longer than anything I did to get me into this position in the first place. Yeah, good old Kurt, the minuteman.

I have to pee again. Damn, I just went on the stick like two minutes ago. Pregnant people have to pee all the time, don't they? Oh, but so do nervous people, right?

I think I'm going to barf.

Oh shit. I got drunk at that party two weeks ago. What if I was pregnant then? What if the baby is deformed or something because of me? I haven't taken my vitamins either. My doughnut and mac-n-cheese diet isn't good for me, much less a baby! I need to buy some vegetables. When was the last time I bought vegetables? They always to turn to mush in the crisper before I get around to eating them. How can I make my child eat broccoli when I find it repulsive myself? It would be so hypocritical! I'm going to make such a horrible mother!

Mother. Mommy. Mama. Oh God, no. That's not me. Not yet.

If I get through this, I'll use three kinds of birth control every single time. Or maybe I'll just swear off sex until I'm married and ready for motherhood. Sure. I could do that. Whatever it takes. Anything to avoid this.

Ding.

To Anyone Concerned

I'm wide awake. It's Sunday night, well, technically Monday morning, 2:47. There's no way I'm getting to sleep. Travis is everywhere, which is ironic because he's nowhere. Wednesday will mark a year since he's been gone. A year of cycling through denial, despair, anger, and regret. A year of berating myself for being blind to the signs that are conspicuous in hindsight, for being clueless about someone I thought I knew so thoroughly. Every day has been darkened by his absence, but I can't wrap my brain around the fact that 363 of those days have piled up in my rearview. The walls of my apartment feel too close, the air inside, too thick and stifling. I need to get out.

I drive to the shop. Everyone is asleep, save for the shift workers and the insomniacs. It's eerily quiet, but in the inky stillness, I swear I can sense the murmur that will gradually become the buzz of the city waking to begin a new week. I already feel less alone.

At the shop, I open the drop box for rental returns during off-hours, take all the bundles out, and bring them to the sorting counter in the back room. There, I wake up the computer, select a bundle, and scan its tag. I squeeze the cord lock to loosen the drawstring and reach inside. Logging returns is tedious, but it needs to be done, and a little mindless work is just what I need right now.

In the first bundle, everything is there: shirt, vest, jacket, pants, tie, cufflinks, shoes, and socks. So many people forget the socks. Far too much of my life has been spent in pursuit of missing socks. I set the shoes and cufflinks aside and give everything else a once-over—looking for damage, checking pockets—before tossing it into the to-be-cleaned bin and opening the next bundle.

If there's anything in a pocket, it's usually a receipt or some tissue, but sometimes there are oddities. A few bundles in, I discover a candy necklace and a little plastic llama inside a pants pocket. Should I bother contacting the customer? It might be worth it, if only to get whatever story is behind this. I'm not calling anyone at this hour, though, so I put the items in a bag and mark it with the rental number.

Checking the contents of the next bundle, I pull a piece of paper from the inside jacket pocket. I'm about to put it in the trash when I see the large block letters: To anyone concerned. More curious than concerned, I unfold the paper and read.

I'm not sure why I feel compelled to write this. Chances are, nobody will read it, at least not in time. At 4:00 Monday morning, I'll be on the Fourth Street Bridge. At 4:01, I'll be in the river unless someone finds this and comes to stop me. If the stars somehow align to make that happen, I'll take it as a sign. Otherwise, goodbye.

I stare at the note, the weight of its meaning settling over me, my face crumpling. I want to dismiss it as a sick joke but can't take that chance. Adding another regret to my already unwieldy load will crush me.

A flood of adrenaline jolts me to action. I cram the note into my pocket and dial the phone number from the rental record. As I listen to the ringing, I grab my keys and rush for the door.

I start my car's engine, and 3:46 glows in blue on the dashboard. The ringing stops. "Hey, it's me. Blah, blah. You know what to do here." Beep.

Who knows if he'll check his voicemail, but I can't not leave a message. "You don't know me, but I found your note, and I'm coming. Just please stay put. I'll be there as soon as I can."

The streets are virtually empty, but I still can't go fast enough. I hit four red lights. As a fifth one looms ahead, I slow down and wipe my brimming eyes to clear my vision. Then I make sure no one is coming and blow through the intersection.

The blue numbers scream 4:00 as I get on the bridge. The clock could be off. This guy has to allow a grace period of a minute or two to account for stuff like that, doesn't he? Knowing he doesn't, I floor it.

I see him—or at least I see someone—on the right side, about halfway across. It must be him. Anything else would be unbelievable in a situation that already borders on impossible. "I'm coming!" I shout. He can't hear me. I lay on the horn.

As I drive the final yards to the center of the bridge, for a second, I swear it's Travis sitting there on the railing.

"Stop! Please! I'm here!" I scream as I scramble out of the car. I can see him better now. He looks so young—early twenties, tops. Not wanting to spook him, I approach slowly. He watches, his face impassive except for a hint of curiosity. I pull the note from my pocket. The wind makes it flutter between my fingers. "You wrote this?"

He moves his head in a barely perceptible nod. "Who are you?"

"It doesn't matter. I'm here."

His eyebrows knit together as he shakes his head. "I can't believe it."

"It's crazy, right? The odds of all this? You've got to take it as a sign. You said you would."

"I didn't think …" His sentence hangs in the air, unfinished.

"There's more. It'll seem even crazier once you know."

He looks skeptical but says nothing.

"Can I just tell you? Can we just find some diner where I can buy you a cup of coffee and tell you everything?"

He looks down at the blackness of the river then squeezes his eyes shut, inhaling sharply. He opens his eyes and exhales. "OK."

The Wedding March

Terrified, she opened the door to step into the church foyer.

"There you are! It's almost time!"

While the first chords of Pachabel's Canon were audible, the foyer was a haze of pink taffeta, white roses, and black tuxedos. Hair was fluffed, and ties were straightened a final time as the party assembled into an orderly queue behind the doors leading into the main part of the church.

Dizzy and parched, she gulped for air, almost inhaling the white mesh that shrouded her face. One hand held the flowers, the weight of which threatened to make her buckle. The other hand was clenched, her perfectly manicured nails digging into her palms until she feared the skin might break. Mustn't get blood on the white dress.

Open and shut swung the doors. One couple disappeared. Her time was scant. The world around her moved in slow motion while her mind was catapulted into the future, revealing a blurry pageant of regrets.

Open and shut they went again. In front of her, only one couple remained. Her feet wobbled in their white satin heels, while the penny in her shoe dug painfully deeper into the ball of her foot.

Open and shut. She was alone, wishing that she loved him.

The music changed—the Wedding March blared to announce the main attraction. Wide open swung the door, and the expectant congregation saw a wisp of white lace disappear out the back of the church.

We All Are Sinners

"So, what's your name?" Father Alberto asked. He didn't actually want to know, but asking seemed like a way to fill the silence as they walked down Chestnut Avenue.

"What would you like it to be?" she said with a look that was somehow half smile and half sneer.

"Mary," he said. "Wait, no, not that. Anything but that." That would be the first name that he thought of, but calling her Mary was just wrong. Who was he kidding? This whole situation was wrong, but he couldn't help himself. He prayed and prayed for strength, but it never made any difference. "Loretta," he said. "Loretta will be fine."

He didn't do this very often—hire prostitutes, that is. Or sex workers, rather—he still wasn't in the habit of using that term. Most of the time, he kept his urges in check, even when Miss Prescott, the volunteer who came in once a week to help clean the church was bending and stretching to get at the dust in all those hard-to-reach places. He could never avert his eyes for long, but he at least managed to keep his hands to himself. Not doing so would mean scandal and humiliation. But every now and then, the urge became so strong that he felt he would burst. If God didn't want him to do this, why would he give him these intense urges that he couldn't ignore? Sometimes he thought it might be a test and that he was failing. If so, it was better to fail with Loretta than with someone like sweet, innocent, lovely Miss Prescott.

"Here we are," he said as they arrived at the gate. He looked around. The moon was full. He would have preferred it to be darker, but, apparently, his libido was not in sync with the lunar cycle.

"You're kidding, right?" Loretta said with a smirk.

"No. Why? What's wrong?" He opened the gate. "I brought a blanket." He held up the backpack he had brought with him.

Loretta wrinkled her nose. "A cemetery? It's a little creepy, don't you think?"

It wasn't the first time he'd gotten this reaction. There had been a couple of girls who flat-out refused to go, but there were others who didn't even bat an eye. He actually kind of liked it when they were least a little hesitant. It meant that they hadn't seen everything yet. And yet, he could usually convince them to go along with it.

"Don't think of it as creepy. Think of it as thrilling."

Loretta raised an eyebrow. "Don't you have a place?" she said. "Or we could go to a hotel if you're married. Hell, even if you have a car..."

She might take a little persuading, but that was still going to be easier and faster than finding another girl. "Listen, it's not so bad, but if you really don't want to do it, I'm sure I can find another girl who would appreciate an extra fifty." He made a show of digging into his pocket and pulling out his wallet. When Loretta didn't immediately respond, he pulled out the two twenties and the ten he'd put aside for circumstances like this.

She looked at the money and clicked her tongue. "Okay," she said and snatched it from his outstretched hand. "I can work with this."

"Splendid," he said as he led her through the gates.

"Why a cemetery?"

They almost always asked, but he never told them the real answer—it was the only place he could perform. He'd tried hotels, cars, trains, public washrooms, playgrounds, and abandoned buildings with only frustration to show for it. He'd never tried a church—that was a line he wouldn't allow himself to cross.

"It makes me feel alive to be among the dead," he said. It wasn't exactly a lie.

Loretta shrugged. "Whatever floats your boat, I guess."

They approached a patch of grass at the north end of the cemetery that was somewhat sheltered by trees and shrubs along the fence. "Here's a nice spot." He pulled a faded yellow blanket out of his bag and spread it on the ground.

"Okay then," Loretta said. She sat down heavily on the blanket. She didn't have a fraction of the grace of Miss Prescott, but she'd have to do for tonight. "How do you want to do this?"

He knelt on the blanket next to Loretta. "First, we pray." He folded his hands and bowed his head.

"Pray?"

"You don't pray?"

"Well, sure, sometimes."

"You needn't pray aloud. Just a little silent prayer before we start."

"Okay."

He saw Loretta roll her eyes before he closed his own and began his silent prayer. Dear Lord, I thank you for bringing me together with this woman. I know you work in mysterious ways and that my actions, although ostensibly despicable, are somehow part of your plan for some greater good. Who am I to question you, oh Lord? However, if I have misinterpreted your intentions and this is not the course you wish me to take, please give me a sign. He waited a few seconds and opened one eye, then the other. There was no sign. Loretta looked at him curiously. He could almost feel her wondering what he had prayed about.

"So," she said. "Now that we've prayed..." She inched toward him. Her voice sounded different. It was lower, sultrier than before—all part of the act.

"Lie down," he said, and she did so.

She was a nice-looking girl. Her hair was wavy and a rich caramel color. Her skin was not too pale, but not too tan either. She didn't wear a lot of makeup—a refreshing change from some of the others. She had a pretty face—not stunning, but pretty—although he guessed she looked a little older than she actually was. Still, she was no Miss Prescott. There could never be another Miss Prescott with her perfect golden curls and peachy skin that made you ache at the thought of touching it. He closed his eyes and pictured her face, her perfect pink lips smiling and her sweet, bashful green eyes. She alone was proof that God existed and was worthy of worship. How unfair it was that he could only admire her from a distance! How heartbreaking that he could only think of Miss Prescott as he inched his hand up under Loretta's skirt and tugged at her panties.

"Unzip me," he said. Loretta fulfilled his request. He buried his face in her neck. She smelled sweet, like lilacs. He moaned softly as Loretta's hand found its way inside his boxer shorts. In his mind's eye, Miss Prescott sipped lemonade while selling raffle tickets at the church picnic. Oh, to be that glass of lemonade and feel the touch of her satiny lips!

"All right, you kids, break it up!" A gruff voice intruded on them, and Father Alberto froze. His eyes opened to a blinding light. Squinting, he held up his hand to shield them, simultaneously realizing that Loretta's thong was still looped around his fingers. He shook it off quickly but probably not before the cop had gotten a glimpse of it.

"Holy Moses! Father Alberto? Is that you?" the voice said.

"Father?" Loretta cried. "Jesus, you're a priest!"

Father Alberto tried to collect himself. He could make out the silhouette of the figure before him now—a police officer. "I—I—I," he stammered. Oh God, a cop—and one who knew him—was this the sign he had asked for? Damn it—it was a little late!

"I'll be darned. It is you," the officer said. "What the?" He aimed the flashlight toward Loretta, who ducked to hide her face.

"Listen, son, this really isn't what it looks like." He had to think fast. There must be some believable explanation. If he could just get out of this, that would be it—no more sex workers. He would get back on the right path.

"Really?" the officer said, moving the beam of the flashlight back and forth between Father Alberto and Loretta. "This isn't a priest getting it on in a cemetery?"

"Heavens, no!" he blurted. But his fly was undone, and Loretta's panties were on the grass next to him. He must have looked like a fool. And if that wasn't bad enough, he was lying about it too! God was vengeful. He'd known all along this was wrong! Why couldn't he have been stronger?

Loretta shook her head. "I don't freakin' believe this. A priest! That explains the praying, I guess."

"You're a fine one to talk, harlot!" Father Alberto muttered and then felt a twinge of guilt. But who was she to judge him?

"Oh, for Christ's sake," the officer said. "She's a hooker?"

Oh, dear. He'd made things even worse, but it hadn't even occurred to him that the officer wouldn't know that the girl was a professional. He'd never even tried to have sex with a non-prostitute. That would be way too much work and provoke far too many questions.

"I believe they prefer the term sex workers now," he said before he could stop himself.

"Thanks a lot, Father," Loretta grumbled.

Father Alberto zipped up his pants and tried his best to compose himself. "Okay, maybe this is what it looks like. I had a moment of weakness. I admit it. I am human. I am a sinner."

The officer shook his head. "I can't believe this. I was one of your altar boys."

Father Alberto squinted. His eyes had started to adjust after the initial blinding from the flashlight. The officer's face did look familiar, but it was hard to be sure in the dark. "Peter McDonald?"

"Officer McDonald," he said gruffly.

"Yes, yes, of course, Officer. I apologize." Caught by a member of his own congregation! There could be no doubt that this was the wrath of God. But God could also be merciful…so maybe there was still a chance he could wriggle out of this. "You know, I haven't seen you at church in quite a while."

Officer McDonald looked toward the ground and rubbed the back of his neck. "Well, you know, I work on a lot of Sundays. I try to get to the Saturday evening Mass at Saint Catherine's, but—hey now! We're not talking about me! You have some explaining to do!"

"Of course. You're right. I'm sorry." It had been worth a try. "As I said, I'm imperfect. A sinner."

"You!" Loretta, who was again fully clothed, sprang to her feet and pointed an accusatory finger at Officer McDonald.

He aimed the flashlight at her again. "Sharon? Oh, God."

"What? Wait a minute. You two know each other?"

Loretta, whose actual name was apparently Sharon, laughed. "Oh, yeah, we know each other. In the Biblical sense."

"Damn it, Sharon! He doesn't need to know about that."

"Know about what?" said Father Alberto.

"You see, Father, Officer Pete here has picked me up a few times for solicitation, but he always lets me go if I give him a little freebie."

"Shame on you, Peter McDonald! You have a wife and child!" Such behavior from one of his own congregation! Had he completely failed them? Of course, there was no denying that this information did offer certain advantages in his present situation.

"Now that I did not know," said Sharon. "Very interesting!"

Officer McDonald put his hands up in front of his torso. "Okay, everyone. Let's just take a minute and slow down here."

"Yes, let's," Sharon said. A devious smile spread across her face.

"It seems we each have a bit of a predicament here," Father Alberto said.

Sharon nodded. "Yup. But it also seems like we might be able to help each other."

Officer McDonald looked curious but wary. "What do you mean?"

"Well, I certainly don't want to get arrested, and I'm pretty sure Father here doesn't either," Sharon said.

McDonald laughed. "Honey, we may have had a deal in the past, but that had nothing to do with Father Horndog here."

"Maybe it's time we make a new deal," Sharon said. "If you let both of us go, maybe I won't tell your wife about our previous meetings."

"Who would believe you anyway?" McDonald scowled at Sharon.

Father Alberto smiled. "If she had a priest to back up her story—say, one who just happened to see the two of you together…" Lies to cover bad deeds would be piling sins on top of sins, but, God forgive him, he had to get out of this. There was too much at stake. He was a good priest. He was a good man. He had but one great flaw.

"Father! How dare you!"

"Don't get self-righteous with me! You aren't exactly innocent here."

"Oh, yeah, Father? How would you like it if your whole flock and the rest of this town knew what you were up to tonight? I can just see the headlines."

My God, what would Miss Prescott think? He could picture the look of horror on her face. No! He could never be responsible for tarnishing that beautiful face by prompting such a look! "I would simply claim that I was the one who caught the two of you together and that you arrested me and made up a whole other story. The word of a cop versus that of a priest—who would people believe? It's a tough call. Of course, if Miss Sharon here were to support my version of the story…"

"Damn straight," she said. "Er, sorry, Father. I mean, yes."

McDonald shook his head. "Unbelievable! You two are disgusting!"

Sharon snorted. "Heck, I just broke the law. I'm the only one here who hasn't broken any vows."

"We all are sinners," Father Alberto said sternly. "But there's no reason these particular sins need to follow us for the rest of our lives." What was important here is that they learned from their mistakes. This might actually work out. God was saving him!

McDonald clenched his teeth and looked at the ground. "Fine," he muttered. "I let you go, and no one says a word about this or about my former dealings with Sharon to anyone, right?"

Sharon nodded. Father Alberto hesitated, suddenly struck—what a wonderful opportunity this was! At first, he'd thought all of this was a sign from God to get him to stop his evil ways, but there was more to it than that. God had led him here tonight to open his eyes to the evils happening in his own community, in his own congregation. His mission was clear now—he must get these sinners to confess and be cleansed. Oh, the Lord works in mysterious ways, but He is good! "Yes, yes. We won't tell anyone—except in Confession! We must all confess!"

McDonald and Sharon exchanged confused glances, but then Sharon shrugged. "Yeah, sure, why not?"

McDonald cleared his throat. "Confess? Hmm... Well, yeah, I suppose I can do that."

"Praise be to God!" said Father Alberto.

When Silence Is Not Golden

They sit facing one another at a small table near the front windows in the coffee shop. He stares intently down at his phone, as if the fate of the world depends upon whatever is displayed on the screen. She is silent, but her scowl beseeches him to put down the glowing rectangle and look at her instead. She sips her coffee. As she returns the cup to its saucer, a bit of the milky-brown liquid sloshes lazily over the side. He glances at the puddle in the saucer, then his eyes travel upward to meet hers. The weak smile that takes shape on his lips begs forgiveness while simultaneously assuring her that he needs to do just one more thing and then she'll have his full attention. His eyes dart back to his phone. Her pursed lips hold back a tirade from escaping her mouth, at the same time betraying her disbelief. She keeps her eyes fixed on him and leans back in her chair. Her bangs flutter in the breeze of her skyward-directed sigh. His eyes have not risen to meet her gaze again, but it's clear that he can feel her stare boring into him as he continues to poke and swipe the screen of his phone. His right leg begins to bounce, its anxious rhythm a percussive riposte to her impatient glare. She picks up her cup and takes another sip, this one accompanied by an exaggerated slurp—rudeness begetting rudeness. He looks at her and sets his phone face down on the table with a flourish, finally finished. Her eyes are weary and unimpressed, but her posture softens. His phone begins to ring, and his body curls in on itself, shrinking. He reaches for the phone with a penitent simper.

Wings

"You get your asses back here!" Dad bellows from the back door.

Brooke and I keep running. He won't follow. He might pass out and forget he was ever mad. Even if he doesn't, his wrath is always more bearable after he's sobered up.

We reach the edge of our back yard and enter the woods with its obstacles and uneven ground. Weaving our way forward, dodging rocks and branches, we barely slow down—we've had plenty of practice at this. Only when we reach our spot, deep amongst the trees, do we stop and gasp, catching our breath.

"I got some new stuff," Brooke says, ducking into our cobbled-together fort—sheets and tarps draped over ropes strung between trees. Inside, we've amassed a stash of miscellanea to help stave off boredom while we ride out these frequent merciless storms. "The library was trashing these."

I eye a faded issue of Quiltmaker magazine in the box she drags from the corner and snort. "Gee, I wonder why," I say as I flump down next to her on the tattered blanket that carpets our sanctuary.

She rolls her eyes as she takes the magazine and tears out two pages. "Here." She hands one to me. "Do like me."

I try to mimic her motions, folding, unfolding, turning, and folding again. But next to hers, my fingers are clunky and graceless.

She finishes by tugging gently at the paper to open its wings. "It's a crane."

I hold up my creation and frown. It looks like someone sat on it.

"You just need some practice," she says through a stifled giggle. "They say if you make a thousand of these, you'll be granted a wish."

I meet her gaze with the faintest of smiles. We have the time. And we both know what we'll wish for.

MICROFICTION

Aha Moment

"Jingle bells. Batman smells. Robin laid an egg." We sing loudly, off-key.

He laughs. "I always thought that was so random. Why does Robin lay an egg?"

"You know… because Robin's a bird."

I swear I can almost see the neurons firing as realization spreads in a slow wave across his face. "Ohhh."

The Beginning of the End of the Line

As the train lurched back to movement, she tightened her grip on the railing, remaining upright despite being jostled. Nearby, a young man rose to offer his seat. Above, a sign read: Priority seating for elderly passengers. She glimpsed her reflection in the window. When had she begun to qualify?

Best Day Ever

She'd been chasing the feeling for decades. Food, gambling, sex, myriad drugs, skydiving, and slacklining all had their merits, albeit with risks. Still, nothing compared.

Everything was simpler back in grade school—before she'd been conditioned to temper her ecstasy. Unfettered, she could revel in the pure unadulterated bliss of Book Order Day.

Big Bad Bastion

"Why are we digging again?" Eins asked, scooping more earth from the trench.

"Yeah," said Zwei, "I forgot too."

Drei sighed. Her brothers weren't the brightest. "The wolf!"

"Where?!" Both brothers frantically looked about.

Drei rolled her eyes. How had they ever managed on their own? At least they'd had enough sense to come here after the huffing and puffing had destroyed their houses. Dim though they were, she'd always love and protect them.

Her brick home, although solid, wasn't impenetrable. But now, with her brothers' labor, the moat was almost ready for filling. Wolfie would never expect the quicksand.

Billet-doux

Nana's clothes were boxed for donation, except the long-coveted cobalt-blue coat, somehow still immaculate after decades. Jenna wrapped herself in its soothing embrace—a perfect fit. Her fingers dipped into the pockets and met paper. It emerged—agedly yellow, glossy from handling.

My Darling Margaret, the letter began. The handwriting was not Papa's.

Blaise the Blasé

Blaise felt vibrations from the oncoming train through the soles of her boots. The whistle sounded.

"Get ready!" Professor Pomp shouted.

"When am I ever gonna need to do this?" Blaise grumbled.

Pomp glowered. "Ever hear of runaway trains, Miss Kent? Not to mention myriad dastardly illegal activities common among rail riders?"

Blaise sighed, crouching into train-stopping stance, wriggling in discomfort. Stupid creeping spandex. The Kal-El Academy uniforms sucked. What's more, despite her lineage and what many called her duty, she had no passion for superheroics. Accounting—that was her true calling. She'd take a calculator over a cape any day.

Bountiful Harvest

I left a bowl of cucumbers on a folding table alongside a sign reading "Free." Someone took the table but left the cukes.

New strategy: I try car doors until I find one unlocked. Surreptitiously, I deposit the produce onto the front seat, shut the door, and walk quickly away.

Changing With the Times

They were a tight-knit group, friends for decades despite wide variations in political views. The agreement to avoid certain conversation topics was key. Some years back, this became increasingly difficult during their monthly card games. Thus, they instituted a new rule: no more games that involve trump cards.

Deathright

Tangled amid the folds of her voluminous cloak, Mortabelle's legs faltered, sending her careening to the pavement. "Ooof."

Gripping the snath of her scythe, she hoisted herself upright. Her target had vanished. Good.

"You let her get away!" her father bellowed. A hood obscured his face, but Mortabelle felt his caustic scowl.

"So what? She's only sixteen!" Such bullshit—to get someone her own age for her first reaping. "Why can't we let her grow up?"

"We don't decide. We simply collect."

Mortabelle rolled her eyes. What a cop-out. Destiny commanded she'd run the family business someday. Then things would change.

Encroachment

Darkness seeps into my mind like gelid air through hidden cracks, devouring joy, sowing despair. Scrambling for a stopgap, I think: kittens.

Endurance

Arm outstretched, she searched for the perfect spot on the rear bumper. She'd made the sticker herself—bold digits 1079 against blue sky and cottony clouds. She'd get questions. Everyone understood what 26.2 meant, but how many people knew the page total for Infinite Jest? She'd inform them. It had been her marathon.

Excavation

As she freed the ductwork segment from its fitting, it slipped from her hands. Amid the dust explosion, something skittered across the floor. She followed it with her eyes, then her feet. Despite a grimy coating, the object's turbinate shape revealed the long-dubious fate of her childhood pet hermit crab.

False Flag

They stand beside their desks, reciting words they know by heart but don't yet genuinely understand. Suddenly, the door swings open. Their pledge to a country that refuses to protect them is left unfinished as chaos erupts. Their hands over their hearts offer no shield from the spray of bullets.

First Impression

"Meet your baby sister!" She holds the bundle out toward me.

Baby sister. These are new words. Curious but chary, I inch closer and catch a scent—new, yet somehow familiar. I soften.

The bundle emits a shriek, blistering and monstrous.

Ears back, I hiss and bolt from the couch.

Found and Lost

A form in my periphery draws my eyes from the flight board, and I see…myself? An exact replica.

Impossible.

But in my core, I know it isn't.

If she's seen me, she doesn't show it. She walks briskly, towing her suitcase. On a mission.

I need to follow her, but I'm stunned, motionless.

I'm jostled sideways as some phone-absorbed guy plows into me. "Sorry," I say—pure reflex.

Glowering at me, he presses forward.

In those precious seconds, she vanished. Frantically, I scan the infinite branches of the concourse for the missing part of me barely realized, now gone again.

Fudging Towards Fate

His profile says he's 35; hers, 34. Both love scary movies, dogs, and stargazing.

They rendezvous over cocktails. Easy conversation meanders toward heavenly bodies, how the return of Halley's comet first sparked their wonderment. They lock eyes. With their fibs exposed, they know their romance was written in the stars.

Goodbye, Girls

They'd been with her through thick and thin, albeit less prominent during the thin. They were part of her—figuratively and literally.

A cheek swab had revealed the lurking threat: BRCA1-positive. At the mirror, she gazed at her unclad torso, bid them a silent goodbye, then donned the hospital gown.

I Want to Break Free

I'm stuck, hung up on this stupid sticky vessel wall in the left leg. Boring! I'll probably dissolve before I get to have any fun.

In daydreams, I break loose and ride the current toward thrilling, exotic locations: heart, lung, brain—places where I can really fuck some shit up.

Infernal Circle

Almost there—just needs a few tweaks.
—Minos

"Sure, just like last time," I mutter through clenched teeth as I click to open the attachment from my editor. My screen is set ablaze with crimson-colored tracked changes and marginalia.

Sighing, I save the file as version 982,451,653 and begin again.

Keeper

She took the shell from the mantelpiece. It had been there forever, part of life's backdrop. Pink- and brown-hued ribbons swirled toward its center. Pretty…but worth saving? Less room for this kind of bric-a-brac at the condo.

They'd begun sorting decades of possessions into piles: "keepers" and "tossers." She wavered between.

His hand reached to guide hers, turning the shell over. On its underside, there was handwriting, faint but unmistakably his. "Holden Beach, 5/15/76."

A tide of memories: Clams and rosé. A moonlit seaside stroll. Their first timid utterances of "I love you."

She leaned into him and sighed. "Keeper."

Like Herding Cats

Some lined up immediately. Others dawdled, compliant but begrudging.

Then, Worry started hopping from foot to foot. Insecurity began to pace. Anxiety spun in rapid circles that would surely induce vomiting. Shame scurried, frenetically searching for a hiding place.

Ms. Brain sighed. Ironic how chaos always erupted during meditation time.

Mind the Wrap

"You traded the cow for *what*?"

Jack winced at the bitter scorn in his mother's voice. He pasted on a meek smile. "Magic bubble wrap!"

She gaped at him with unvarnished chagrin. "And how, pray tell, will a scrap of packing material put food in our bellies?"

"It grants wishes. One for each bubble we pop—twenty-five of them! Here..." Jack turned and reached toward the tabletop where the precious sheet of plastic should have been.

From underneath the table came a rapid series of snaps, then delighted squeals from his little sister as twenty-five ponies materialized inside the tiny cottage.

Misspelling

The spell called for moonfish, but tuna would have to do—supply chain issues. She stirred it into the cauldron while reciting the incantation and picturing her beloved becoming warm again, suffused with life, coming to embrace her.

She waited.

Her withering jade plant revived to a vibrant green.

Ontogeny

Last year, she'd imagined placing herself inside a paper bag with a banana. Just the way it turned mangos tender and fragrant, it would spur her development. She'd catch up with the other girls. Now under continual assault by leering eyes, she wished for that paper bag to hide inside.

Overzealous

The tinny melody finds our ears. "Ice cream!" we squeal through unfurling grins.

Granny supplies the funds. Drumstick for Chris, pushup for me. Licking eagerly, I inch the sherbet cylinder skyward, taunting fate.

Powerless, I watch its slow-motion topple. Despair, a creamy orange puddle, bleeds outward on the hot pavement.

Pitch Din

That.

Damn.

Sound!

Continual but intermittent, like Chinese water torture.

I can't find the source. What's worse: nobody else seems to hear it.

They're gaslighting me—just like with the Where'd the ball go? trick.

Time for retribution! Clutching their car keys in my jaws, I head for the garden.

Prospecting

I wake to find ten dollars under my pillow.

All day, my tongue probes for potential cash, prodding each remaining tooth, hoping for a hint of wobbliness. Nothing budges.

Daddy's dozed off on the couch. He's got loads of teeth! I sneak off to his workshop to find a hammer.

Regret

"I miss you!" he called from the living room.

She rolled her eyes. She'd been gone for 20 seconds and was one room away.

Making the love potion had been easy. Brewing the antidote was much more complicated—it had taken months. She uncapped the tube and reached for the wineglass with the chipped base.

His arms encircled her from behind. Startled, she jumped. The open tube tumbled into the sink.

Rescue Cat

Princess Aven rolled her eyes at the gamboling jester.

Queen Laelynn glowered. Her realm was withering under a blistering heatwave—cursed by Magus Petroleus. Only fourteen-year-old Aven's laughter could lift the spell, but hundreds of hopefuls had roused nary a smile. "Next!"

A mousy girl curtsied in greeting.

"Well?" Laelynn huffed. This didn't look promising.

From her pocket, the girl produced a small rectangle and held it up to reveal moving pictures on its surface.

A portly ginger tabby wriggled its way into an inordinately tiny box.

Aven's lips twitched upward. She giggled. Relief, a cool zephyr, swept in.

Suspension

Through the tangles of hair thrashing her face, she glimpses something yellow in her periphery and turns toward it: a handmade sign taped to the pylon.

Need help? A phone number.

Fingers stir inside her pocket, seeking her phone. The bridge will still be here later if she needs it.

Tidy Tree, Straggly Apple

"Do you need to have all your cash organized just so in your wallet?" Mom smoothed out the bills, orienting them faceup, arranging them by denomination.

In my wallet, crumpled bills mingled with receipts and oddments, hastily stuffed inside. Mom knew this. Yet she always asked, probably hoping the answer would someday change.

Vigil

"Count sheep," he said. "Never fails."

But she kept losing count, backtracking, stressing.

Now, she holds a tally counter, pressing its lever for each member of the wooly herd until her hand eventually falls slack with sleep.

Beside her in the darkness, he listens; each click another water torture droplet.

POETRY

The Ballad of Belle Gunness

Norwegian-born near Selbu Lake in 1859
Although she came from modest means, Belle grew robust and fine
In 1881 she crossed the ocean with desire
To find wealth in America, to lead a life less dire
Chicago-bound was this young belle; there Sorenson she wed
They opened up a little store, sold sweetmeats, ginger bread
Alas, a fire destroyed the shop, which had not seen success
Insurance payout saved the day! For Belle was truly blessed
A happy pair they must have been 'til some years later on
One summer's day, he met his end, Belle's dear Sorenson
Cause of death: his heart had failed, though some declared foul play
They said that Belle with strychnine had put Sorenson away
The timing of Belle's husband's death it seems was just too apt
Twice-insured he died the day those policies o'erlapped

But Belle unscathed, no charges filed, she took her windfall dough
She moved to Indiana next and found a brand new beau
The widower Pete Gunness soon made Belle his blushing bride

But happy times turned sorrowful when Pete's young daughter died
And such bad luck, more came so soon, just eight months down the line
Poor Pete met an accident—was burnt by scalding brine
To make things worse, some heavy gear from on a nearby ledge
Crashed down on Pete and hit his head, or so Belle did allege
This time folks just would not buy the tale that Belle had spun
Demanded further inquiry so justice could be done
The coroner reviewed the case, and murder he decreed
But crafty Belle convinced the cops that she'd done no misdeed
Some years passed uneventfully, on second thought, not quite
Belle's foster daughter Jennie seemed to disappear from sight
Belle said that she went off to school, although this was a lie
The truth remained a secret, which I'll tell you by and by

In time, it seems Belle got to be quite lonesome on her farm
She cast a net through personal ads to emphasize her charm
Comely widow seeks to meet a gentleman upright
With view of joining fortunes, thus in marriage to unite
Glib responses Belle insisted she'd not dignify
She stated this quite plainly so: Triflers need not apply
And suitors soon began to come from places far and near
To win Belle's hand, to demonstrate intentions so sincere
One named John arrived to prove he'd outdo other men
Within a week, he disappeared, was never seen again
No one can say with confidence how many came to call
We might in fact need several extra hands to count them all
A man whose name was Anderson was lucky you might say
For he alone escaped Belle's trap—the one who got away

Meanwhile Belle did curious things; she ordered hefty trunks
So many it's unlikely they were just for storing junk
What then could their purpose be, and might that be connected

To tales that some began to tell of sights quite unexpected?
Folks passing by the farm at night had claimed they'd spotted Belle
In the hog pen toiling, digging, why they could not tell
Still all the while more suitors flocked; one from Wisconsin came
A well-appointed widower; Budsberg was his name
Last seen alive inside a bank obtaining wads of cash
And signing over deeds to land—an act some thought quite rash
In time his children worried, wondered, wrote to Belle, inquired
Had their father been to visit? If so, what had transpired?
Belle's letter of reply composed, and it was quickly sent
With deep regret she told the children she'd not seen this gent

We can't forget Ray Lamphere—hired hand on Belle's estate
With Belle he grew quite smitten, and his jealousy was great
When callers came to visit Belle, he'd get in quite a snit
At last one day Belle fired him, saying he was most unfit
But Lamphere would not stay away; Belle said he caused her strife
She told anyone who'd listen then that she feared for her life
And rightly so perhaps, you see, for late one April night
The Gunness house was claimed by fire, burning fierce and bright
A body in the ruins lay, found absent of its head
Even so, townsfolk assumed that Belle was surely dead
And Lamphere was the culprit; he'd clearly set the blaze
So he would sit in prison the remainder of his days

All around much gossip spread, and rumors they did fly
About the things that might be buried out in Belle's hog sty

And when police began to search, what ghastly things they found!
Bodies, some in parts, some whole, buried underground
Perhaps a dozen, maybe more, there were so very many
And as you may have guessed by now, indeed, they found poor Jennie
You might think it served Belle right to burn up like she had
Not so I fear! For I have just a little more to add
Exactly what became of Belle, no one can say for sure
But that body in the ashes found, we now know was not her
Although that corpse was badly burned and lacking head and neck
Its measurements did not fit Belle's when someone thought to check
There long persisted gossip of Belle sightings far and wide
Quite tantalizing rumors, yes, but never verified

We'll never know with certainty the number that Belle killed
Some put the total over forty graves this wily woman filled
It seems unjust that such an awful villain got away
Then again, by now she's dead I think it's safe to say
But let us not take too much peace and comfort in that thought
Mankind it seems has endless stores of evil to be fought

The Ballad of Herman Mudgett

This story, I will tell you now
And leave you then to judge it
Born in 1861
Was Herman Webster Mudgett
You might not recognize the name
But you may know his story
For many simply can't resist
A tale so strange and gory

Of his early years of life
Not very much is known
New Hampshire is where he was born
And lived until he'd grown
At seventeen, he met a girl
Clara, whom he wed
And his new wife, conveniently
Had quite a lot of bread

This money funded Herman
While he studied in med school
And meanwhile, by 'most all accounts
He treated Clara cruel
Eventually, the two split up

But never did divorce
And Herman's life began to take
A much, much darker course

While in school, he launched a scheme
He pilfered from the lab
Cadavers he then claimed as kin
Insurance fraud cash-grab
After Herman's graduation
To Illinois he came
And there he took another wife
Myrtle was her name
Bigamist this made him then
Oh, but never mind
Of all his wrongs, this one is small
I'm sure you soon shall find

As criminals are wont to do
Herman changed his name
H. H. Holmes, he dubbed himself
Ere he rose to fame
Or infamy, more apt a term
For such a man so ghastly
Around this time, by most accounts
His deeds became quite nasty
A pharmacy in Englewood
Is where he took employment
And ladies flocked there just to flirt
With Herman for enjoyment

When the drugstore's owner died
Holmes arranged to buy the store
But the widow got no money
And then was seen no more
A vacant lot across the street

Herman also bought
A boarding house, he thought would be
Well-suited for the spot
The World's Fair in Chicago
Would be commencing soon
Visitors would come in droves
And bring Herman quite a boon

For boarding house construction
Many builders Herman hired
But after just a week or two
Most were usually fired
By this method Herman could
Cheat workers out of wages
But also made sure that the house
Was built in finite stages
This was crucial to ensure
No one could recognize
The full extent of evil plans
That Herman did devise

"The Castle" Herman dubbed the house
And when it was complete
What it held in store for guests
Was anything but sweet
Hallways wound and snaked around
As if to make a maze
Some stairways led to nowhere
Leaving many guests quite fazed
Hidden chutes and trapdoors
Soundproof, sealed-tight rooms
Some had gas jets; folks within
Could not escape the fumes

The basement Herman kept well stocked
With tools and key supplies
To deal with those unlucky guests
Who'd meet their grim demise
One device, a kind of rack
Which Herman had invented
Stretched their bodies till they broke
The victims he tormented
Vats of acid, quicklime pits
Surgeons' tools galore
All a budding psychopath could want
Was surely kept in store

Some victims he persuaded to
Send loved ones correspondence
Telling of their travel plans
And thus explain their absence
Some bodies Herman stripped of flesh
And with the bones remaining
He reconstructed skeletons
Sold to schools for training

Holmes went on this way for years
His murders undetected
How could it be for all that time
That nobody suspected?
Then again, perhaps some did
Surmise that Holmes was vicious
And likely he was quick and sure
To silence those suspicious

If all of that was not enough
Holmes hatched another plan
Insurance scam; he'd pull it off
With Ben, his right-hand man

They conspired to fake Ben's death
Holmes said he'd have no trouble
He'd get a corpse resembling Ben
To stand in as his double
With the body's face disfigured
The truth would be obscured
Insurance payout on Ben's life
Then would be assured

As always, sly and cunning
Holmes betrayed his faithful friend
Attacked Ben in his room one night
And brought his life to end
For some time Holmes kept up the ruse
Assuring Ben's dear wife
That Ben was hiding out; soon would come
They payout of their life

And with this final crime it seems
That Herman's fate was sealed
For not much later, he was pinched
His butchery revealed
Arrested, tried, convicted
And there sentenced to the noose
Holmes would finally get his due
For all his crimes profuse
No one can say with certainty
How many Herman slew
Twenty-seven, he confessed
But later claimed just two

In May of 1896
Holmes took his final breath
At Moyamensing Prison
Where he was hanged to death

By his request his coffin was
Encased in thick cement
And buried all of ten-feet deep
Graverobbing to prevent

For well more than 100 years
Conjecture was persistent
That Herman had escaped somehow
So many were insistent
They said he bribed a prison guard
To help him dodge the noose
Another convict hanged instead
While Herman was set loose
Some said he went to London
And there continued killing
Becoming known as Jack the Ripper
A thought that's surely chilling
Down to South America
Some people said Holmes fled
And lack of evidence will seldom
Halt a rumor's spread

And then in 2017
Plans were at last laid out
To get conclusive answers
To erase remaining doubt
Scientists began to work
They dug for three whole days
An empty coffin then was found
Much to their amaze
But soon the scientist figured out
That this was just a ruse
A decoy to make would-be thieves
Befuddled and confused

And so, the crew resumed their work
Removing still more ground
And reached what they had sought at last
Another coffin found!
Unlike that empty first, this box
Contained remains indeed
And for their age, quite well preserved
Those present all agreed
For on the face of those remains
I swear that this is fact
Was Herman's trademark, bushy, full
His mustache was intact

To prove for certain it was Holmes
And put all doubt to rest
The scientists took samples
Seeking DNA to test
From three of Holmes' descendants
Genetic samples were obtained
So their relation to the corpse
Could then be ascertained

But testing DNA so old
Is quite an undertaking
Few labs have the means for this
A process quite painstaking
The first results returned, alas
Were sadly inconclusive
Answers after all this time
Might prove to be elusive
Further tests would be required
While Holmes' descendants waited
Would DNA show them to match
Or were they unrelated?

But after several months, the lab
Provided affirmation
The remains and Holmes' descendants
Had familial relation
So, Holmes had not escaped, it seems
He finally got his due
Though one could argue he deserved
Much worse for all he slew
Of all that can be said of Holmes
This cannot be denied
His life and crimes have fascinated
Many far and wide

Now that you have heard this tale
You may be filled with dread
Thinking of such ghastly deeds
Such horror and bloodshed
And you may well be wondering what
Could make a man this way
Though guesses we may hazard
For sure, we cannot say
But Herman's explanation
For whatever that is worth
He claimed he'd had the devil
Inside him since his birth
And whether you believe
In devils, demons, or in hell
Holmes surely proves that evil
Lurks among us where we dwell

Better

Like everyone else, I'm afraid
For myself – just a little
For those I hold dear – much more
And for countless others I'll never meet
The threat of this viral menace
Looms large over all

I do what little I can
Stay at home, wash my hands
Wear a mask, keep my distance
Hang onto hope that we'll weather this storm
Together but apart
And perhaps emerge better

Meanwhile, there lurks
Disquiet within me
Relentless whispers
That this may be just what we deserve
Not individually, but
Collectively, as humans

Our mighty race
With dominion over earth
Behold our achievements!

Rape, torture, murder, enslavement, destruction
No virus can outrival
What we inflict on each other

I want to believe
We're worth preserving
We can learn and be better
But a cursory look through history suggests
Supporting evidence
Is, sadly, sorely lacking

The insidious, insipid source
Of our downfall
Might merely be this:
Few are at fault, yet all are complicit
Perhaps what remains when we're gone
Will be better

Crossroads? (A Golden Shovel Poem)

I cannot help but think, has it come to this?
Are these strange times an omen, cryptic as it is?
Could this turn of events finally be the
indisputable evidence that we the people have lost our way?
Or might it instead be something more uncertain, the
proverbial turning point that will seal the fate of the world?
For better or worse, will we find that the ends
do indeed justify the means, although it may not
be apparent as we live in the moment, laden with
so much turmoil, confusion, and injustice looming in a
stifling cloud? We feel powerless do anything but bang
our heads against metaphorical walls. But
still, somehow, all the while, we continue to harbor a
quiet sliver of hope, even as we whimper.

This is the way the world ends
Not with a bang but a whimper
- from The Hollow Men by T.S. Elliot

Four Days in November

1
Tuesday
Election Day
But I voted days ago
Not for my ideal
But at least for
The lesser of two evils

Nothing to do now but wait
For those first creaks and cracks
Melodic clinks of falling glass
Later, as the map turns crimson
Confidence yields to disquiet
The fate of the union
Undetermined
By the time I land in bed

2
Wednesday
Alarm ends my fitful sleep
I grab my phone
Check for news

Gape in disbelief
Dissolve into sobs
Helpless, hopeless
Powerless to devise a reason
To rise from bed

Weep, wallow, repeat
Unable to comprehend
How
Or fathom
Why
My fellow Americans
Would choose to empower
Hatred and bigotry
Or at the very least
Look the other way

3
Thursday
Tears stay at bay
But my eyes
Still swollen, still raw
Betray the despair
Of someone lost
In the only home she's ever known

Am I so out of touch?
Sequestered in my bubble?
A blue island
Amid a sea of red
This world I now behold
Seems unfamiliar, peculiar
Am I seeing clearly
For the first time?

4
Friday
Still terrified, still irate
Incensed, betrayed
Paralyzed, impotent
Yet desperate to act
I open my purse
Give what I can
To preserve priceless liberty

I don my safety pin
Then second-, third-
And fourth-guess this gesture
Solidarity or self-soothing?
Both?
The pin stays, for now
And I vow not to stop
Searching
For ways, large and small
To rise up
To go high

I Am From

I am from all-copper pre-1982 pennies
saved in large coffee cans
from Noxema and mosquito punk sticks
I'm from a bedroom with lime-green shag carpet
yellow and white gingham wallpaper
(décor so loud it's a wonder I could sleep)

I am from maple tree helicopters
and towering spruces
in whose branches at night
I swore I could see the face of a witch
I am from Saturday morning cartoons
and Sunday morning pancakes

I am from frugality and laughter
from a farm-boy dad and a city-girl mom
who raised small-town kids
I am from sweet corn
and homemade chocolate chip cookies

I am from Jeepers cats! and Are we having fun yet?
from the Golden Rule and Think for yourself

I'm from ribboned barrettes and friendship pins
from roller-skates and saucer sleds
snow forts and Big Wheels

I am from trips to the beach with grandma and cousins
Jolly Good soda for all
A t-shirt over my bathing suit as SPF
I'm from summer road-trip family vacations
in a car with no a/c
(On one trip I got chicken pox)

My mother lovingly pried fading photos
from self-adhesive albums
whose glue was now brittle
scanned each one into bits and bytes
digitally preserved memories

My brother and I time-travel
traversing decades over cocktails
and conversations
where every sentence seems to begin
Remember that time…

Memento

On a sultry night
late in summer
when one could easily forget
that the weather will soon turn cool
my eyes follow
its yellow-green glow
zigging and zagging across the yard
until it flits
to somewhere beyond my sight

At the time
I don't know it
but I've just seen
my last firefly of the season
and now I wish
I could remind myself
to savor the moment

Paradox

If you're not a writer
You don't know contradiction
All at once loving and hating
Adoring and loathing
This endeavor, this hobby
Or, for those lucky-unlucky few
This profession

If you're not a writer
You don't know incongruity
This habit, this addiction
Is part of your identity
You can't imagine stopping
Yet sometimes find it
Nearly impossible
To begin

If you're not a writer
You don't know dissonance
Simultaneous fear that
You have so much to say
But nothing worth hearing

Desperate longing
To have your work read
And paralyzing fear
That people will read it

If you're not a writer
You don't know disharmony
Knowing since you were small
Just what you wanted to do
Exactly what you wanted to be
And in some ways, already were
Yet knowing you needed
A backup plan
Grounded in reality

If you're not a writer
You don't know discord
Swelling with pride
Seeing your work in print
But aching with want
To take it back
Revise it here, tweak it there
So it could be better
And you could truly be proud

Sister

We have been friends
Seemingly forever
Certainly longer
Than either of us like to admit
Different mothers, different fathers
But sisters nevertheless
I can scarcely believe I lived
Almost eighteen years before knowing you
Before we put our heads together
And made the "mind-meld" noise
Somehow, we both instinctively knew

When you told me about the cancer
I cried and cried
And then chided myself
For not being the pillar of strength
That you might need
Although the prognosis was good
I let myself think just for a second
Of life without you
And I could not breathe

You will be okay
Because I said so
Because you have to be
There is no other option
The position of my best friend
Has been forever filled

Some day, when our hair is gray
And we are older than we'll ever admit
We will sit in our rocking chairs
Or perhaps on barstools
Sharing stories told a thousand times over
Better and more elaborate with each telling

Roommates as fire hazards
Houseguests who won't leave
Landlords who would have us
Shower in the dark
But sleep with the lights on
Dodging our own proverbial bullets
Feeding marshmallows to alligators
And using coconuts as sound effects

Then
When we stop laughing
And feel good and rested
We will rise
Give each other that knowing glance
And set off together
In search of more tales to tell
Capers to be thoroughly lived
And retold with embellishment
Ad infinitum

Tabula Rasa

The screen is blank
Save for the cursor
Which blinks
Daring me to begin
Urging me to wield my power
To create
To destroy
To give life
And to take it away
With deft keystrokes
Cities are built
Or bombed into oblivion
Love blossoms
Or wickedness prevails
Characters thrive, prosper, exalt, rejoice
Or they endure, suffer, weep, whimper
All depending on
How I
The writer
Feel today

To the Unconceived

How can I
Create
Something I may
Resent
For stealing
My time
My sleep
My very sense of self
And even my
Love?

Not to bring you into
Existence
And risk
Remorse
For what might have been
Is better
Than to burden you
With my own
Regret

Unsung

Love is in the mundane
Where you might not think to look
Patient, steadfast, and true
Hidden in plain sight

When grand romantic gestures pause
You'll find love folding laundry
Or cleaning out the litter box
Love is in the mundane

At times, the lead at centerstage
More often love's the stagehand
Behind the scenes or in the wings
Where you might not think to look

Sometimes love's the melody
But oftentimes, the drumbeat
The rhythmic throughline of the song
Patient, steadfast, and true

Seek love within the masterpiece
Reflected in the backdrop
Find the artist's hazy visage
Hidden in plain sight

Waking

her leaden eyes open slowly
as she emerges
from vaguely angry dreams
with a tense and qualmish feeling
she knows
she will not shake until midday

while the warmth
of her most recent lover
still lingers in the bedclothes,
she is already beginning
to forget his name

NON-FICTION AND HUMOR

A Brief Bio Statement for Query Letters to Literary Agents

My writing has appeared in *The New Yorker*, *Harper's*, and *The Atlantic* under the pen names Joyce Carol Oates, John Irving, and Margaret Atwood. I am fluent in more than a dozen languages, including three that I created myself. I have guessed every Wordle correctly on the first try. Five of my phone doodles hang anonymously in the Louvre. I have memorized pi to more than 7,000 digits. In my spare time, I create satirical and cryptic street art under the pseudonyms of Banksy and the Toynbee Tilemaker. I had a perfect attendance record throughout my 20 years of schooling. I can fold fitted sheets flawlessly with ease. I served as a model for both the Gerber baby and the Columbia Pictures torch lady. The Dalai Lama occasionally asks me for spiritual advice. I am immune to the common cold. I always know the exact time without having to look at a clock. I have been employed as a pilot, a snake milker, a pastry chef, and a spy (the latter two simultaneously). I have devised cures for three types of cancer and dandruff. I invented the semicolon, avocado toast, and flossing (the viral dance craze, not the dental hygiene practice). I have deciphered the Voynich Manuscript and identified the sources of the Wow! signal, the Taos hum, and Havana syndrome. I can hold my breath for more than ten minutes. I have beaten Lebron James and Michael Jordan at HORSE. My shadow puppetry is world renowned.

However, I have yet to realize my dream of publishing a novel.

Dear Anne

"I don't want to have lived in vain like most people. I want to be useful or bring enjoyment to all people, even those I've never met. I want to go on living even after my death." –Anne Frank

Like so many others, I read your diary when I was young. I was with you as you talked about treading lightly so that the workers in the factory below would not hear you. I felt your longing to go outside, to breathe the fresh air and feel the sun on your face, to be free again. I marveled at how upbeat you often seemed in spite of your circumstances, how you still believed that people are good at heart. And I wondered as I read, could I have done the same? What would my diary have looked like if I had been in your shoes?

I visited your house on my birthday. Some might consider that that odd, but thinking of you reminds me that life should be celebrated, for it is fleeting.

I saw the place where a bookcase concealed the entrance to your secret dwelling. I stood where you hid, where you slept and dreamed, where you wrote. I saw the walls that kept you safe but at the same time kept the world out and imprisoned you. I looked at the pictures that you pasted up on them, the movie stars and the clippings of Princess Margaret and young Elizabeth, who would be Queen in just a decade or so. I took all of these in, somewhat surprised to find that, although you clearly were extraordinary, at the same time you were still a normal teenage girl.

I saw photos. You smiled at me from your writing desk and I smiled back. I think you would have liked that. But in the next moment, I choked back tears, thinking what a shame it is that such a lovely, smart, thoughtful young girl was never allowed to finish growing up. I am quite certain that you would have been an even more lovely, smart, thoughtful woman.

I read your names and those of your family members on the pages of the ledger for the camp, and the horror wound its way through my veins and filled my heart. When I thought about how your story is just one of the few that we know well—one tragedy among millions more that will never be told, I could hardly bear the thought. So, instead, I focused on your wish and how it came true. Your life was far too short, but you live on. A girl like you who has touched the hearts of so many can never really die.

Dear Len

February 8, 2017

Dear Len,

You inconsiderate selfish bastard! I'm not normally a violent person, but I'm so furious I want to punch you. Of course, I can't do that, so this letter will have to suffice. If there is something after this life, maybe you'll read it. I hope so because I have a lot of things to get off my chest.

Angry as I am, I'm also really sorry. We used to be so close, but the years passed, miles got in between us, and we drifted, as people often do. It wasn't anyone's fault—it was just life happening. Still, I can't help but wonder whether things might have turned out differently if I'd made more of an effort. I'm not self-centered enough to think that what you did had anything to do with me, but that doesn't mean I can easily dull the chorus of questions rattling around in my brain. Would it have mattered if I'd tried to be a better friend? What if I'd done more than send the yearly holiday card and click like or make the occasional comment when you shared pictures and stories on Facebook? Was there anything I could have done that would have prevented this? Anything that would have let you know that, despite the way our lives diverged, you were still special to me? Could a well-timed call or text message somehow have made the difference between your doing what you did and hesitating, calling someone, anyone, for help? And if so, how the hell was I supposed to know? That's a big-ass burden to place on anyone, and I'm just one among the many people you had in your life. What if all your friends had tried a little harder? Would that have changed things? What if you had somehow been able to glimpse the future to see how we'd all react—the grief and the awful hole you left in the lives of those who loved you? Would that have made you reconsider?

I realize I'm asking impossible questions. I'm also looking for rational explanations where there probably are none to be found. What you did wasn't rational. And again, I get the urge to smack you for being an irrational thoughtless jerk. Then I feel guilty for being mad because I know—maybe not fully, but I have some idea. I know how depression can take you to depths that feel so utterly hopeless that you can scarcely imagine ever feeling happy again. When I think of the despair you must have felt, my heart breaks. Whatever demons you were battling were so fearsome, so brutal, so merciless that they made you believe ending your life was not only an option but the best option at your disposal. I'm not sure if I can fathom how intense your misery must have been for you to make that choice, to leave behind your wife, your boys, father, sister, and friends. Your agony had to have been unbearable, and I hate that you had to feel that way even for a second, but that doesn't make what you did okay. What you were feeling, as horrible as it must have been, was temporary. What you did was permanent.

I was trying to recall the last time we saw each other, and I'm not even sure. Was it at your wedding reception, or was there another time after that? Someone else's wedding or some other festive occasion? In any case, I prefer to keep my memories of you aligned with happy times. I'll picture you wearing one of your crazy shirts or some whimsical tie grinning that goofy grin of yours, and I'll know, or at least I'll hope like hell, that your smile was genuine, that there was some real joy in your life. Then my heart will ache at the almost impossible thought that I'll never see you again, and I'll hold on tightly to those memories.

So, where am I going this this? Hell if I know. I just needed to write it. Maybe it doesn't make a lot of sense, but what you did doesn't make sense either, so don't go pointing fingers. I know things will get better with time, but my wounds are still fresh, and I guess I'm trying to sort out my mess of feelings. Perhaps this letter is really my way of saying goodbye since I didn't actually get that chance. My life was better for having you in it. I miss you more than I ever realized I would. I'm still pissed at you, but I also hope you found some peace.

Love,
Liz

Dear Writer's Block

Dear Writer's Block,

I hate to do this in a letter, but I've been over and over it again in my head, and I believe it's for the best. This letter itself means I'm writing again, so you probably already know what I'm going to say. Things just aren't working out between us. Don't get me wrong, we had our good times together—playing silly computer games, checking FaceBook, shopping, going out to lunch. You were even there with me when I resorted to rearranging the cabinets and cleaning out the junk drawer as a means of procrastination. Even though part of me was having fun with you, deep down, I knew it wasn't right. I shouldn't have let it go on so long.

When it all began, you were just an escape, but then things started to get more serious. I could tell you were getting very attached, and for a time, I thought I was falling for you. But slowly, I began to realize that the hold you had on me wasn't healthy. You said that you only wanted to make me happy, but what you offered was merely empty distraction. I could feel you holding me back, preventing me from realizing my potential and fulfilling my dreams.

It was the last straw when I found out about the others. Yes, I know about the DePaul student whom you took to all those frat parties when she should have been working on a paper about Proust. I also know about that so-called journalist from the RedEye who was forever shirking deadlines to be with you. There were probably others. You'd think I'd be angry, and at first, I suppose I was a bit. I'm glad now, though, because I have finally realized that it's time to let go.

I think all along we both knew that we weren't meant to be and I would eventually have to return to my first love, Writing. And so I am. I'm not going to lie and say that we should stay friends. That just wouldn't work. We need a clean break. With that, I wish you well and say goodbye.

Resolutely,
Liz

The Definitive Guide to Writing the Perfect Query Letter

If you have aspirations of publishing a novel, you might think that once you've finished writing the manuscript, you've conquered the hardest part. Although this is a great accomplishment and an important step, it's a relative piece of cake compared with what lies ahead. To realize your goals, you'll probably need to secure representation by a literary agent, and for that, you'll need a query letter. You may have heard that the agent query letter is the most important letter you will ever write, and likely rewrite upwards of 17,500 times. If you peruse enough advice about query letter writing, you might be led to believe that the query is more important than the novel itself and perhaps start to wonder why you bothered to write a novel at all. But well, you did, so you should craft the best possible query letter to give your novel its greatest chance.

There's no shortage of advice on writing a query letter that will capture an agent's attention and hold onto it like it's the last available package of toilet paper in March of 2020. I know this because I've read pretty much all of it. Plus, I've combed through hundreds of successful query letters and drafted countless versions of my own. And since I've done this, you don't have to. I've distilled my massive collection of knowledge down to this handy guide. Let's dive in!

The Opener

Begin with a simple salutation: Dear XXXX, for example. But include the agent's name in place of the XXXX. Never use a generic salutation like Dear Agent or even Dear Exalted Literary Gatekeeper. The agent is taking time from their busy schedule to read your letter, so the least you can do is address them by name.

There are two main schools of thought as to what should directly follow the salutation.

1. The Hook

   This is the all-important sentence that will grab the agent's attention and make them start panting in anticipation. Opinions vary as to what should go into a hook. Many describe a hook as a one-sentence summary of the most unique and interesting elements of the novel. Others say that any number of things can comprise a great hook: compelling information about you or your book, particulars on the book's target market, a relevant quote or statistic, or even a string of seemingly random words, provided they are expressed with gusto (SHOEBOX ARMADILLO CHEESE PANTS!)—anything goes as long as it's attention-grabbing. If your query letter doesn't begin with a fantastic hook, you put the agent at risk of dropping dead from boredom induced by your dreadful, tedious nonhooky text—and who would want to represent someone who did that to them? So, obviously, the hook must always follow the salutation, unless of course you belong to the other school of thought.

2. The Setup Sentence

   For every literary professional who insists the hook must come first, there's another who is just as adamant that

> query letters must open with a simple statement of the letter's purpose (i.e., that you're seeking representation for your novel), then provide the title, genre, and word count. Without this setup, the agent might become confused, unsure why you're teasing them with (albeit fascinating) nuggets of a story about Emile, a flying badger with the power of telekinesis. Who would want to represent someone who disorients them by wantonly lobbing plot points without a bit of setup first? The nerve!

Unfortunately, you might not know which school of thought your prospective agent subscribes to. Thus, you must simultaneously take both approaches. For this, I suggest a Choose Your Own Adventure structure.

Sidebar: Does anyone like rhetorical questions?

Absolutely not—rhetorical questions will brand you as an unsavvy neophyte. Agents are dead tired of this tactic—except those who say it's fine if it's done well (whatever that means).

Personalization

Agents receive gajillions of query letters each nanosecond. To make yours stand out amid the slush, you should personalize it toward your prospective agent. Ideally, you'll have had some personal exchange you can mention, but if not, don't panic—you can still personalize your letter if you do some research. The agent's profile on their agency's website is likely to be chock-full of information about their education, storied career, hobbies, condiment preferences, blood type, and sports team allegiances. Oddly enough, the profile may offer little hint as to the types of manuscripts they are seeking, but there are plenty of other sources you can tap for that:

QueryTracker, Manuscript Wish List, and Publisher's Marketplace, to name a few. Follow the agent on Twitter and/or Instagram. Stalk them (from a distance). Go through their trash. Channel all the informational tidbits you gather toward personalizing your query letter because doing so is vital—except of course when it isn't. Many agents say that, although a previous personal connection is worth mentioning, beyond that, personalization isn't likely to make or break your query. Some agents even note that going to extreme lengths to personalize a query can sound contrived. So, don't try too hard to personalize. Except do—because it's vital!

The Summary

Your query letter should include a summary of your novel, providing a sense of the story and overall themes without describing every plot point, spoilers and all. Most guidelines suggest this should be limited to a few sentences, definitely no more than one paragraph. Yet, in my review of successful query letters, I've found many with plot summaries that spanned three or more paragraphs. So...go figure. Keep it as brief as you can, I guess.

The Bio

There are several important do's and don'ts when it comes to bios.

- DO mention past publication credits if you have them. These tell the agent that someone found your work worthy of publishing, which will give you a leg up...maybe. Has your work appeared in publications everyone in the solar system has heard of? If so, great! If not, it's either still great because every bit helps, or it's not worth mentioning because no one except maybe your mom cares about the story you had published in obscurity. Many literary agents are open to working with new authors, so you shouldn't worry if you haven't published anything yet...probably. It depends. Have you been trying to get published for decades to no avail? That doesn't mean you're a bad writer, just that your writing hasn't found the right home yet—unless of course you are a bad writer. On the other hand, maybe this novel is your first attempt at getting published. That's no problem whatsoever, but it does signal to agents that you have no idea what you're doing and aren't especially dedicated to your craft.

- DO mention interesting details about yourself if they are relevant to your novel, unless they're weird and off-putting (the exception here being if you know, through your stalking and trash research that the agent is into things most people find weird and off-putting). Do you have experiences and/or hobbies that provided special inspiration or insight for your book? Mention those in your bio. But be careful not to mention too much. As I noted earlier, agents read megabazillions of query letters. So, if yours is a single character longer than necessary, it's liable to make the agent's eyes bleed. Then the agent will do everything in their power to ensure you never succeed in your literary endeavors.

Comp Titles

Numerous guidelines advise mentioning a few recent books that are comparable to your novel (aka, comp titles). A lack of comp titles suggests that there is no market for your book and your quest for publication is hopeless. However, many guidelines suggest that comp titles aren't critical and should be mentioned only if they have been published within the past five years, have sold well, and are very closely aligned with your own in terms of tone and structure, in which case they render your book superfluous. So, to recap: Mention of comparable books is necessary but unimportant. Comp titles indicate that there's an existing market for your book while simultaneously demonstrating that your book is redundant and therefore unmarketable.

The Closing

Most commonly, a synopsis and the first 10 to 20 pages of the manuscript should be included with your query letter, but each agent/agency has specific submission guidelines, so it's important to check these and follow them precisely. Wrap up your letter by stating that you have included whatever is indicated in the guidelines. Many sources suggest mentioning that you would be happy to send the full manuscript on request. Others advise against this approach since (*eye roll*) duh. Either way, close by thanking the agent and signing off.

And that's it! Simple, right? Not at all convoluted and rife with conflicting advice! Now, go forth and query!

Dream Players

Scott

My first love. Together, we felt everything with the ferocity of youth, before life had taught us to stifle our feelings, tamp them down lest we find ourselves depleted, exhausted by the weight of our own unrelenting emotions. Intensity like that isn't sustainable. Neither were we. And so came my first true, crushing heartbreak, an agony scarcely matched since then. For a while, I tried to convince myself that I hated you, but I never did—not really. Regardless, I let go of any bad feelings long ago, holding the good ones in the chamber of my heart reserved for the fond memories of so many firsts. You don't visit my dreams often, but when you do, the frisson of youth returns to me. Heart stirring, head light, I'm exhilarated and terrified, as if standing on a precipice, unsure what will happen but knowing that whatever does will be foundational to who I am. In those dreams, sometimes, we're as we were back then: young, quixotic, and passionate. Sometimes, we're older, meeting again somehow, decades later. Always, I'm willing to risk heartache, knowing that the rush and rapture of young love are more powerful than the fear of a broken heart can ever be.

Garret

From first grade through high school, we were classmates, acquaintances but never truly friends. I haven't seen you since graduation day, and I'd seldom thought of you until some years back when, inexplicably, you began to crash my dreams. Several times a year, you turn up in my slumbering mind, appearing in scenes that are always variations on the same theme. Circumstances throw us together, and we clash, bickering and sniping, delighting in each other's chagrin Yet, beneath our mutual disdain for one another lurks a sexual tension like that seen only in movies. We try to resist, but it's futile. When we give in, it's frenzied, typhonic, carnal, and always exquisite. I wake up sweaty, breathless, and perplexed. Why you? Why has my subconscious cast you as the star in some of my most salacious dreams? Have I ever crept into someone's psyche and assumed such a role? Have I been in your dreams?

Ben

We were never good for each other, but when has that ever mattered to those who are young, idealistic, and fiercely in love? When I finally began to realize just how bad for me you were, I was stuck. I sometimes imagined a better life for myself, free from you, but I couldn't find the path there. So, for years, I stayed with the devil I knew, miserable inside the prison of my own making. When finally, I tried to escape, my first attempts were unsuccessful. You used every device in your manipulative toolkit to reel me back in. But eventually, with time and struggle, I cut that line and broke free. Now, decades later, you still plague my dreams. The details differ, but the story is always basically the same: We are together. I want out. But I can't seem to tell you, or you refuse to listen when I do. So, I stew amid the urgent longing to be free from you, my panic growing with each passing moment. When I wake, relief spreads through me in a slow swell of realization: It was only a dream. Yet again.

Logan

Only the bizarre logic of dreams could allow me to believe the awesome revelation that you are still alive. You had never died—that was just some terrible mistake. In other dreams, you're just there, and thoughts of your death couldn't be further from anyone's mind. The last time you graced my dreams, we sat around someone's dining room table to play some silly game that involved plastic fish, laughing, buoyant. And when I came back to consciousness, the loss of you hit me anew, fresh and cutting after all these years. Nevertheless, it was good to see you again, dear friend.

Ethan

Each of us in an unhappy coupling, we sat side by side late into many a night—partners in research, perpetually on the verge of something more. Casual touches and glances lingered as we told each other and ourselves why we shouldn't, why we couldn't. We should have. And every now in then in my dreams, we do.

Note: Names have been changed to protect the innocent (and the not so innocent).

The Elephant on the Lawn

In the fall of 2008, as my father raked leaves on the front lawn, he bent to pull his Obama/Biden sign out of the ground. The election was over, and the sign, a standout symbol of liberalism in the conservative sea of Southeastern Wisconsin, was no longer relevant. As he stood and tossed the sign aside the pile of collected leaves, a neighbor happened by.

"Well," he said to my father, amiably, but with a slight edge of unhappiness. "Your guy won." He motioned to the sign on the ground.

My father nodded and smiled, not being one to gloat.

"I can't say I'm too happy about that, but we'll see how he does," the neighbor continued. "I'm sure glad that Proposition 8 passed in California, though."

If I had to guess, I would say the neighbor wasn't trying to start an argument or raise a controversy. Perhaps he even said it in hopes of finding some common ground with my father. In 2006, Wisconsin had amended its constitution to prohibit gay marriage, and I would wager that, in the town where I grew up, the vast majority of inhabitants who voted supported that ban. So many other people in town would have nodded in agreement, smiling as they bonded over the thought of denying rights to their fellow humans. Others may not have agreed with the neighbor's sentiment but would likely have changed the subject, not wanting to make a fuss.

Little did the neighbor know, he'd hit on a hot-button issue, and his comment would not be left unchallenged. My dad, who is normally quite mild mannered, threw rake to the ground in disgust. "Are you kidding me? That just makes me sick! Why in the world would anyone see such blatant bigotry as a positive thing?"

The neighbor's mouth hung open as the worms continued to emerge from the can that he'd opened, and my father continued. "What business is it of the government or anyone else who a person wants to marry? Did you happen to think for one second how you might feel if a close friend or family member, or even you yourself were the one having their rights stripped away? No, you probably haven't even considered it, but you know what? I have, and frankly, anyone who sees my son or my son-in-law as a second-class citizen can go jump in a lake!"

I don't know if my dad's rant changed the neighbor's mind. I'm guessing it probably didn't, but maybe it made him think just a little bit more about why he had the opinions he did. That may not seem like much, but it's a step. A mind must be opened before it can change, and then, the change doesn't occur in one fell swoop, but in a series of small steps. Transforming society happens even more slowly, but each step is an important one.

Perhaps other people would have remained silent on the issue, either to avoid confrontation or out of a hopelessness that the neighbor's opinions were too deeply etched in stone, but my dad resisted such cynicism. He refused to remain silent and took the opportunity to face the issue head on, attempting to chip away at that stone.

My father, my hero.

A Host of Problems

"So, you're making your first communion soon?" Shane, a fifth grader, said as he approached a group of us second-grade girls one day at recess.

Fifth-grade boys usually didn't talk to second-grade girls unless they meant to torment them, so we were wary. "Yeah," said Megan, the boldest among us. "So?"

Shane bounced a basketball slowly and tossed it over to Randy, another fifth grader. "I'm just curious. Have the priests and nuns have told you everything?"

"Of course," said Megan.

I wasn't so sure. "What do you mean?" I squawked.

"They didn't tell us everything before we did it, right, Randy?"

Randy grinned slyly and bounced the ball back to Shane. "They sure didn't."

"What are you talking about?" Megan sniffed. She was trying to brush this off, but she was obviously nervous.

"I don't know if I should say."

"They'll find out eventually," Randy said.

Megan rolled her eyes. "You're just trying to scare us."

I couldn't speak for everyone, but the scare tactics were working on me. I was worried enough about tripping on my way up the aisle and about whether my soul was pure enough to receive Jesus. Adding the thought that the grown-ups were withholding some important detail made me wish I was Jewish.

"Oh, just tell us!" said Mary, another girl in the group.

"Do you think they can handle it?" said Shane.

Randy shrugged.

"Just tell us or leave us alone!" Megan said. She crossed her arms in front of her chest defiantly.

"Okay, I'll be nice and warn you," Shane began. "You know during Mass, when the priest says all of that stuff and the bread changes into the body of Christ?"

"Duh," Megan said.

Shane stuck out his tongue at Megan before continuing. "When you take communion, you'd better not bite or chew."

Randy snickered. "Not unless you want a mouthful of blood."

"What are you talking about?" Megan sounded less confident.

"The host will bleed if you do," Shane said.

"No way!" Megan said, her voice faltering.

"It's true alright," said Shane. "I just wanted to warn you. No one warned us, and boy were we surprised!"

I told myself that Shane and Randy must be messing with us. There was no way the grown-ups wouldn't have warned us. Then again, some churches gave out wine with communion, which was supposed to be Jesus' blood, so maybe the adults figured it was no biggy. Still, the thought of having something start bleeding in my mouth was enough to make me lose sleep. I didn't even like hamburgers unless they were well done. Plus, even if I didn't chew or bit the host, wouldn't it start bleeding when it got all smooshed up in my stomach? What if I got sick? Everyone would think I was a bad person because Jesus made me sick!

The next time I was in church, I watched closely at communion time. Sure enough, most people didn't chew. They just held a serious look on their faces and eventually swallowed. But there were a few who walked back to their pews chomping away. Unfortunately, everyone had enough manners to chew with their mouths closed, so I couldn't tell if there was any blood.

I thought of asking my parents or a teacher about it, but I couldn't bring myself to. If Shane had been lying, I'd look stupid. If he'd been telling the truth, I didn't know what I'd do. I couldn't not go through communion. It was supposed to be all wonderful and holy, but I dreaded it.

At my first communion, I didn't dare bite or chew, and I managed to choke down the host without retching. It just tasted like stale bread, which gave me hope that Shane had lied. Still, I'd have to take communion at least once a week for the rest of my life. How could I do that unless I knew? I had no idea what I'd do if a bite of host sent blood gushing into my mouth and trickling down my chin. Perhaps I could fake illness until I found a different religion to convert to.

Gradually, I worked up my courage to find out the truth. I chickened out several times and swallowed the host after it got mushy on my tongue. But finally, one day as I walked back to my pew, I bit down tentatively but firmly. No blood squirted. Nothing felt or tasted different. I bit down again. Nothing. To be sure, I feigned a sneeze and spit into my hand. I folded my hands in prayer but discretely peered between them to check. No blood. No gore. No Jesus guts. I quickly wiped my hand on the tissue in my pocket and breathed a sigh of relief.

How Are You?

People ask me this frequently. To be clear, I'm not talking about the congenial but perfunctory inquiries of grocery store cashiers or baristas, voiced mainly out of habit or a need to fill silence. The queries I refer to come from people I know, some from acquaintances, others from close friends and even family members. I have several stock answers.

- *I'm hanging in there*
- *Could be better, could be worse*
- *OK…considering*

These responses might not provide a lot of information, but they have to suffice because really answering the question is way too complicated. It would take a long time, and I don't think it's what people really want when they ask. It's not that I suspect people ask about my well-being only to be polite—I do think they are genuinely concerned about my condition. It's just that they want the Cliff's Notes version of the answer, which is fine because usually, neither they nor I have time for more. So, I usually give one of my canned responses. It's easier. Besides, when it really comes down answering the question How are you? the truth is, I just don't know.

In many ways, my day-to-day life hasn't changed since I was diagnosed with breast cancer. My time is still filled with work, household chores, and hobbies. Granted, I rest more often, and in any given week, I almost always have at least one appointment with some doctor or another. I don't look that much different. My wig resembles my pre-cancer hair reasonably well, and I didn't lose weight on chemotherapy like a lot of people do. There are a few differences, though. I often look tired, and I feel like this whole thing has aged me, but then again, I started out looking young for my age, so I guess I've got that going for me. If you look closely, you might notice my eyebrows are drawn on since my real ones have become quite sparse. The biggest differences, though, are not obvious to the casual observer. I'm not talking about the physical effects of the cancer itself or the gallons of poison I had pumped into my veins during months of chemotherapy. Neither am I referring to scars from biopsies and surgery. I'm talking about the mental differences.

When I think back, even though it was only about 6 months ago, my pre-cancer life seems like a different planet—one I wish I could visit, if only for a little while, a vacation from cancer if you will. The first few weeks after I got the news were a frenzied haze of disbelief, anger, and fear. I wondered if there would ever again come a time when I wasn't terrified all the time. Thankfully, that changed as I received more information, a prognosis, and a treatment plan. After some of the initial fear subsided, I was revved up and ready to fight. I couldn't wait to start treatment—I was going to kick the shit out of this thing that was trying to take over my body.

Chemo was rough. Really rough. At times it seemed endless. But before long, I could literally feel my tumor shrinking, and I clung to that knowledge when I was feeling my worst. I sometimes wonder what I would have done, how I would have felt if I hadn't known the chemo was working. On top of the fatigue, the nausea, the hair loss, the blisters on my hands and feet, and the fact that everything tasted off, what if I also had to deal with constant paralyzing fear like what I'd felt just after my diagnosis? How would I handle that? I guess I'd find a way because it's not like there's an alternative. Several people remarked about how brave I've been through all of this, but I don't see it that way. I've simply been playing with the hand I was dealt. I haven't endured chemotherapy and surgery out of courage, just out of necessity. My sense of self-preservation kicked in and keeps me going, even though the uncertainty of the future I'm heading toward scares the hell out of me. At this point, I'm reasonably confident that I still have a long life ahead of me, but I feel like I can't conjure a clear picture of what that life might look like, which is s scary in its own way. I'm pretty sure my life will never be the same as before I was diagnosed. Some things will seemingly return to normal. My hair is starting to grow back, slowly but surely. Some day, I'll have real eyebrows again. The sutures from my surgery will heal, and the scars will grow fainter over time. For a while, a daily commute to receive radiation therapy will become my new normal, and after that, I'll have years of anti-hormone therapy and whatever side effects accompany that. But I wonder, if and when all this is over and I beat this thing, who will I be without cancer?

On some level, I know I'm much more than my cancer, but it's so easy to lose sight of that when something takes over your life the way an illness like this tends to. Certainly, having it take over my life beats the hell out of having it take my life, but it's scary not knowing what the future will look like. Will my identity shift from cancer patient to cancer survivor? In forming our identities, we choose some things—writer, vegetarian, cat person, knitter, Cubs fan. For others, we have no choice in the matter, and sometimes those shift abruptly, like when I found myself going from healthy woman in the prime of her life to cancer patient in the blink of an eye. I certainly never wanted to define myself by a disease, but cancer is insidious. It has a way of creeping in, inserting itself into your identity, much like the malignant tumor proliferates and displaces healthy tissue. You hate it, but it's a part of you, and even if you think it's all been cut out, there could still be small bits of it lying in wait. Imagining life without cancer becomes almost as difficult as wrapping your mind around your own death. Ostensibly, it would be just like before you were born, but somehow, it just doesn't compute.

So, how am I? It's just so hard to say. Perhaps it's too soon to tell. Maybe I should just give one of my stock responses and not think about it too much while I simply continue to play the cards I've been dealt. That's all any of us can really do.

Hypothetically Speaking

I love hypothetical questions. There's something fun about musing over how I might handle predicaments that are unlikely ever to present themselves. If nothing else, our answers to such questions tell us a little something about ourselves. A friend once asked me, if I could only have one condiment for the rest of my life, what would it be? I can scarcely imagine how I would encounter a situation in which my condiment use would be so drastically limited, and if I ever did find myself in such a position, it's even harder to believe that I would be given my choice of condiment, rather than having, say, mayonnaise (ew!) forced upon me. Of course, the fact that all of this was highly unlikely didn't stop me from mulling the question over for some time and deciding on salsa.

So, what psychological insight can be gleaned from my condiment choice? You might just think that I like salsa a whole lot. Indeed, I do, but you would probably be surprised to learn that I actually like mustard better. However, instead of impulsively answering the question based on my deep love of mustard, I considered my options carefully and chose with the condiment that, not only do I like a great deal, but also, in my eyes, is a more versatile and more sensible choice in the long run. I am nothing if not a planner.

More than once, I have been asked, if I could go back in time and change one thing in my past, what would it be? Obviously, this would be impossible, unless there have been some pretty exciting breakthroughs in quantum physics that are being kept under wraps. Still, I'm as much of a sucker for a time travel story as I am for a hypothetical question, so I consider the query, and one thing always comes to mind immediately. If I could go back in time, I could avoid ever talking to a certain guy (we'll call him Jake) who I met in college.

Jake and I had a tumultuous relationship from the start, and it only got worse from there. When I think back to that time in my life, I'm actually embarrassed that it's me in my memories. I want to smack my past self. How could I have let myself get into such a mess, and why the hell did I stick around for three years? I can blame it on the folly of youth, say that I am older and wiser now, and remind myself that hindsight often makes things much clearer, but I still find it hard to fathom that I could stay with a man like Jake for so long. Was my self esteem really so low? Did I just not know what a good relationship was like? There were so many red flags. Did I really not see them, or did I just ignore them?

I probably had more than my share of your typical late teens/early twenties angst, and I felt like a little bit of a failure because, while most of my friends had long-term boyfriends, I'd never had a relationship last more than a few months before Jake came along. Jake was passionate, artistic, contemplative, and charming. I was taken in by him before I realized he was also manipulative and emotionally unstable. He used my insecurities to his every advantage. He loved me like no one else ever could, or so he said. If I wanted to spend time together while he was in the wrong mood, I was smothering him, but if I went off without him, he was angry and suspicious.

Once, Jake and I were out to dinner with some friends. At one point, I unknowingly upset him, and without a word, he got up from the table and left. Everyone had assumed he'd gone to the bathroom, but he never came back. When I returned home, after paying for the lobster he'd ordered but never eaten, I found my apartment in shambles—broken picture frames, clothes strewn everywhere, books dumped off their shelves. Jake had torn my home apart, all over something that turned out to be a misunderstanding on his part. But you see, he'd reacted so strongly because of how much he loved me and how passionate he was about me. That was what he claimed, and I fell for it.

Whether his manipulations were intended, just a symptom of his own psychological instability, or a bit of both, I don't know, but they continued right up until the end. When I finally broke up with him, he threatened suicide. When that didn't work, he said he still wanted me in his life and that we could be friends, and then he stalked me.

I wouldn't wish what I went through with Jake on my worst enemies, yet, when I start to think of changing the past, it opens up such a flood of questions. If it hadn't been Jake, who's to say it wouldn't have been someone else, maybe even someone worse? What if my meeting Jake that night so long ago meant that I didn't leave the fraternity party early and ultimately prevented my being hit by a car on the way home?

The simple fact is, I have no idea what my life would be like if I hadn't been involved with Jake. It might be very different—perhaps better in some ways and worse in others—but I'll never know. It would be easy to look back and regret that I ever met him, ever spoke to him, or ever loved him, but it does me no good. We can't change the past, so the best we can do is learn and grow from it. My time with Jake may was hellish in many ways, but I know I am stronger person because of it. How can I regret something that has made me stronger and wiser? Even in hypothetical musings, I know that everything in my life has made me the person I am today. So, there will be no going back and changing the past, even hypothetically, because I like myself…even more than I like mustard.

The Joy of Socks

It's time for me to admit I have a problem. In the grand scheme of things, it's not a terrible problem, but I can't ignore it anymore, so I'm going to own up. If I have been even moderately diligent about keeping up with the laundry, my sock drawer is overstuffed to the point that I can't fully close it. The issue actually first reared its head a few years ago when I was keeping my socks and my tights in a single drawer—that this was once possible seems amazing to me now. I deferred the problem by transferring my tights to a storage box that now sits beside my dresser. Alas, that too is now overflowing. In the interest of full disclosure, I should also mention that holiday/season-themed socks (e.g., those depicting pumpkins, witches, reindeer, snowflakes, and the like) are in separate storage and are unearthed when seasonally appropriate.

I don't recall exactly when my sock preoccupation (or presockupation as I have come to call it) began. I didn't just wake up one day, suddenly sock crazed. I don't remember being particularly sock focused in my younger days. I had the basic neutrals—black, navy, grey, brown—and I usually had a few pairs with stripes, argyle, or polka dots to jazz things up. Occasionally, as a gift I'd receive a pair with something a little nuttier, like a zebra print. At the time I probably wouldn't have thought to buy such socks for myself, but those gifts would always bring a smile to my face. I think that was when I started to get hooked.

A dozen or so years ago, I was in Target (a perilous place, a veritable minefield for anyone with even the slightest tendency to make impulse purchases) when I spotted a pair of socks on an end-of-aisle display. Their predominant pattern was black and grey stripes, but these weren't simple straight stripes. Rather, they were somewhat curvy and irregular, like the stripes of a tabby cat. Up at the top of the socks were adorable cat faces, one on each sock. I stopped for a moment, smiled, and continued on with my shopping excursion. Yet, as I got my vitamins, conditioner, and laundry detergent, my mind returned to the socks. They were kind of perfect. Most people would just see the stripes, which were kind of funky but still basically neutral-colored stripes. But above those stripes, hidden by the sock-wearer's pants, the cute silly kitty faces would lurk in covert whimsy.

Eventually, I had made a loop around the store and was back near the socks. I paused for a second but passed them by again. Nah, I don't need them, I told myself as I headed toward the checkout counters. I was kidding myself. After about fifteen paces, I turned abruptly, went back, and grabbed the socks.

Those were my gateway socks. I began a wild ride down the slippery slope of sock addiction, which happened to coincide with an explosion in the whimsical sock industry—or so it seemed. Perhaps an endless array of kooky sock options had always been available, but I hadn't noticed them. Quickly, I began to realize that, for any aspect of my personality I wished to express, there was a corresponding pair of socks. For instance, if you didn't know I was a writer, you might figure it out by looking at my feet on any given day because I have socks with motifs of typewriters, pencils, books, and library cards. I have one pair where one sock has the full titles of once-banned books and the other has the titles blacked out, as if they had been attacked by a censor with a thick marker. I've got socks from New York, Paris, Amsterdam, Alaska, Hawaii, Napa, and Dublin. I was dismayed to come home from a recent trip without having found a pair of Luxembourg-themed socks. I have socks with hot air balloons, wine bottles, musical notes, galaxies, narwhals, and Rosie the Riveter. I even have a pair of socks with pictures of shoes on them. Ironically, I don't have any sock-print socks, but I have no doubt that such things exist. I've got socks with colorful patterns along with fun sayings like "Duchess of Sassytown" and "Let's carpe the fuck out of this diem." I have three pairs of socks that identify me as a badass. Shortly after I was diagnosed with breast cancer, a friend bought me a pair of hot pink socks that depict a purple cat flipping the bird and proclaiming, "Fuck cancer!" I wore those socks for every one of my chemo treatments.

Even with my wide and varied collection, I know I've barely begun to scratch the surface of the novelty footwear world. I've learned that there are at least ten different sock subscriptions services, and although I have not (yet) joined any of them, it feels good to know they're out there. It lets me know I'm not alone in my presockupation. Frankly, as addictions go, this one is fairly benign, but, as they say, admitting you have a problem is the first step in dealing with it. So, yes, I admit it. I have a problem: I need a bigger dresser.

Just Be Happy!

"Maybe it's time for you to consider treatment with an antidepressant."

The words weren't exactly a surprise to me, but they still made me cringe. Antidepressants were for two kinds of people: the lazy ones who took the easy road of popping a happy pill and ignoring whatever was wrong in their lives and the weak people who just couldn't handle life. Either way, taking these pills represented some kind of character flaw, a moral failing even. I should be stronger. I should be able to cope. I shouldn't curl up into a ball and cry when I get stressed about work or when I can't find my other sock. If I needed antidepressants just to feel normal, I must be bad.

Weak.

Broken.

Useless.

Bullshit.

Too many people view the body and mind as two distinct entities, when they really aren't. They're irrevocably linked, if not one and the same. My brain is part of my body, after all. My brain does not make enough serotonin, and that makes me, at times, physically incapable of being happy. But there's a treatment, and once I stopped listening to all the bullshit and took antidepressants, I felt like the person I had actually been all along finally got to come out.

Still, some might say I shouldn't need these pills, that they are a crutch in the worst sense of the word. "Happiness is a choice," the saying goes. I should just make myself be happy out of sheer will. Just be stronger. Just be more positive. Just be happy!

Just start making insulin.

Just stop releasing so much histamine when you encounter pollen.

Just build stronger tooth enamel.

Just stop refluxing acid into your esophagus.

Just stop breaking down cartilage in your knees.

Just stop growing tumor cells.

Sounds simple, doesn't it?

The Kid Question

My wedding day was one of the happiest days of my life. It was lovely in pretty much every respect. After all, it's not very often that I get to dress up in a beautiful gown, have just about everyone I love in the same room, and dance the night away with my friends and family. Combine all that with the fact that I was legally united to the love of my life, and it was as close to perfection as any one day can get.

That was also the day when people stopped asking me the question that I had been hearing for five years or so: "When are you going to get married?" The question had many variations (Why haven't you two gotten married yet? Do you think he's going to propose soon? Are you ever going to get married?), but it was essentially the same. Happily, I knew I would not be hearing it anymore.

Of course, that question was promptly replaced by a new one. I had been expecting it at some point—I would have been naïve not too, but I have to admit to being a bit surprised when it came not fifteen minutes after Ian and I had tied the knot.

"So, when are we going to start seeing some little Liz's and Ians?" a family friend asked at the cocktail hour that immediately followed our wedding ceremony.

Humor, preferably of the sarcastic ilk, really is the only appropriate response to a question posed in such a manner, especially when the ink of the signatures on your marriage license is not yet dry. "I'm sorry, did you want us to slip into the coat closet and get started on that right now?" I said with a sly grin.

Although I laughed off the question at the time, I knew that it was only the beginning. "When are you two going to have kids?" was what most people were going to be asking of me sooner or later.

What bothers me most about this question is not that it's intrusive. Although my reproductive status is not really anyone else's business, I suppose I can understand the curiosity to some degree. What bothers me about the question is that it is so presumptuous.

I'd be much more amenable to the question if the when were excised from it. With one simple editorial change, the question goes from presupposition to merely curious inquisition. But, alas, the when is almost always there.

The when bothers me on a couple of different levels. First of all, how do the posers of this question know that I am able to have children? Do they never consider that I may desperately want a baby but am having fertility problems, and, by asking, they are bringing up what is almost certainly a touchy subject?

As it happens, that is not the case with me, but it brings me to my second problem with the when. Why do people automatically assume that I want and intend to have children? Why is the predilection toward procreation considered to be the default state of a married couple? According to the National Center for Health Statistics, the percentage of women aged 15 to 44 years in the U.S. who were voluntarily childfree rose from 4.9% in 1982 to 6.2% in 2002. It may be a small minority, but it's a growing one.

I have several stock pithy responses to the question (We're waiting until we can get one on sale. Oh, crap, I knew there was something we were forgetting to do! When we run out of other things to do and talk about.). However, when such replies escape me or if I am not feeling especially sarcastic, I will answer the question honestly, and say, "Actually, we're not sure if we want kids."

In rare cases, the poser of the question will nod his or her head and say, "Ah, well, don't have them unless you really want them," (now there's an idea!). But more often, my answer educes a condescending look that says, "Oh, sure you don't," or the inevitable follow-up question is posed: "Why not?"

I can think of any number of reasons why I might not want to have children (e.g., I like my life the way it is now; children are messy, expensive, and energy-sapping; the world is already overpopulated; I want to devote myself to my career; I love that things in my house do not mysteriously become sticky while I'm not looking). However, I simply don't understand why I must justify my indecision on the matter.

Upon hearing that someone I know is expecting, I have often been tempted to ask her why she wants a child. Thus far, I have held my tongue, as I'm sure that asking such a question would be considered brazen and possibly offensive. Actually, it's none of my business why other people feel the need to breed, but if I do think that if you are going to bring a life into this world and take on the responsibility of caring and providing for it for 18 years or more, you should probably have some darn good reasons for wanting to make such a mind-blowingly huge commitment. But most people don't think of it that way. Of course everyone wants to have children—they are a joy! Yes, I'm sure they are the epitome of bliss, except for the pain of labor, sleepless nights, thousands of dirty diapers, need to brave holiday shopping stampedes for this year's must-have toy, constant worrying about their well-being, being subjected to Shrek III roughly 900 times, tantrums, the rebellious teenage years, and skyrocketing college tuition costs. Yet people often react as though there is something wrong with not wanting children and that choosing not to have them would be condemning myself to a meaningless existence. Thankfully, childfree people tend to have more free time, disposable income, and rewarding hobbies; these saving graces, along with being better rested than your average parent, help us muddle through our meaningless existence.

From the time that I myself was a kid, I expressed doubt about whether or not I ever wanted kids. Every time, my musings were met with the same reaction: "You'll change your mind. You'll want kids one day."

Well, I'm coming up on 35, and I'm still not sure that kids are for me. I won't say absolutely not, but at this point, it's not looking good for anyone who is rooting for me to breed. These days, people do take me more seriously when I say I'm not sure that I want kids, but that doesn't necessarily mean that they accept my answer happily and without further comment. "Oh, but you'd be such a great mom!" Based on what? My fear of change or my lack of experience in caring for children? "Don't you think you'll regret it some day if you don't have them?" Perhaps, but that's a heck of a lot better than having children and then regretting it.

The strangest people are those who see my lack of desire for offspring as some sort of personal affront, as if, by not having kids, I am suggesting that people who do have children made the wrong choice. That is simply not true. The path you choose may not be right for everyone, but that does not mean it is not right for you. So, please, if you encounter me or any other childfree person, put your assumptions aside. After all, if you stay on our good side, we might baby-sit for you some time when you need a break from the little ones.

A List of Possible Reasons That More of My Work Has Not Yet Been Published

- I don't know the right people. You have to know someone on the inside to really be successful at this game.
- Editors and publishers have bad taste.
- My work just isn't that good.
- Let's be honest, I'm a little bit lazy.
- I'm subconsciously sabotaging myself because I have a fear of success.
- Making a living off of my creative writing has always been a pipe dream.
- The general public has even worse taste than editors and publishers. Just look at some of the stuff out there that sells!
- I simply haven't yet written the story that will open the floodgates of my success.
- There's some sort of conspiracy against me. People who I suspect may be involved include Lady Gaga, Ann Coulter, my ex-boyfriend, and Amy, that bitchy waitress I worked with one summer when I was in college.
- Bad karma.

- Unfortunately, I'm one of those people whose true genius will not be fully realized until after I'm dead.
- Someone somewhere has cursed me.
- It's totally normal to get a lot of rejections, and I shouldn't even start complaining about it until I've gotten at least a hundred more.
- I waste far too much time puttering around on the Internet when I could be writing.
- People are intimidated by my good looks and my unique sense of style.
- My writing is so smart that it goes over the heads of most people.
- My writing is not actually as smart as I think it is.
- The economy—it's hard to sell anything these days.
- My work is too good for the publications that I've been submitting to; it would put everything else they publish to shame.
- Cubs fans can never win.
- I'm not British. This is really neither here nor there, but part of me has always thought that my life might be better if I were British.
- Becoming a pastry chef is my true calling.
- Chuck Norris has threatened to kick the ass of anyone who publishes my work.
- All of my e-mail submissions are being intercepted by gremlins that add the words snickerdoodle, parsimonious, and blubber to every third sentence of my stories.
- People have become so accustomed to crappy writing that they don't even know what to do anymore when they come across good writing.
- It's better this way. If people start reading all the things that I've written, they will realize how twisted my mind can be.

- Everyone hates a vegetarian.
- Becoming a well-known, highly regarded writer would make my life just a little too perfect.
- Nargles.
- I've neever ben grate at prooffreadding my own work.
- My shameless flouting of superstitions has caught up with me.
- I have a problem with follow through. I start a lot of things and don't

The Little Blue Book

Even before I knew how to read, I liked the idea of books—their look, their smell, the crack of a new binding, their weight in my hands. The den in my childhood home had bookshelves built into the walls, not a vacant space among them. I would select books from the ones I was able to reach and simply page through them. I knew my ABCs and could recognize letters, but I was not yet able to decipher the words. Nevertheless, I knew there was something special and exciting about books, and I could hardly wait to be a part of it.

I listened intently when parents read to me from Dr. Seuss, Little Golden Books, Richard Scarry, and the like. I also had picture books that came with records. A gentle-voiced man would read the book's story to me, and a bell would sound when it was time to turn the page. Although I loved those books and their stories, I wanted more. Those thin, colorful books didn't satisfy my need for something I couldn't quite identify but associated with the more substantial volumes that graced my parents' shelves.

I fell in love with one book in particular. It was heftier than any of my picture books but still of manageable size for the four-year-old that I was. It was hard backed and covered with bright blue cloth. I loved to run my fingernails along the cover, feel the vibration, and hear the wick-wick noise that it made. I would sit with the book, pretending to read it, turning pages after whatever I deemed to be an appropriate amount of time had passed. I carried that book with me wherever I went and professed to whomever inquired about it that it was my favorite book. That declaration was usually met with a chuckle, although, at the time, I didn't understand why. I don't recall exactly when, but eventually the chuckles made sense when I realized that the little blue book I loved so much was 50,000 Words Divided and Spelled. The book contained no great adventure story, no fable from which to draw a moral, no heroes living happily ever after, but that hardly mattered to me. I had already succumbed to the allure of books. And once I learned to read, things only got better.

Mind Your Dots: A Public Service Announcement on the Responsible Use of Ellipses

We must act now to prevent a catastrophic punctuation crisis!

Dwindling supplies

- According to the Society for Appropriate Punctuation, the global supply of ellipses reached critically low levels during the last quarter of 2021
- If ellipsis use continues at present rates, supplies could be totally depleted before 2025
- The US has a small cache of ellipses on reserve for emergency use, but access to that supply will be restricted to government officials and high-ranking military officers

Causes of the shortage

- Massive increases in the use of ellipses have been recorded since the advent of the internet
- In 1985, on average, each American used just ten ellipses per year
- By 2015, that average had ballooned to 743, with most ellipses being used in work-related emails and social media posts

Economic impact

- All those unnecessary pauses add up!
- In the US alone, the annual cost of superfluous pause–related lost productivity resulting from improper ellipsis use has risen steadily during the past four decades and is currently estimated at $175 million

What will happen if the global supply of ellipses is depleted?

- Without ellipses, writers will be unable to add critical pauses to their work
    - Characters will be unable to have their sentences—or even their internal monologues—trail off; their only hope for leaving a statement or thought uncompleted will be an interruption (e.g., from another character, an explosion, or a wayward mongoose), in which case an em dash can be deployed
- There will be no more anticipation dots for people to fix their gazes upon while waiting for a response to a text
    - This will leave texters with no way to gauge the amount of time their text partners spent typing a response, tinkering with it, deleting it, redrafting it, and scrapping it again before finally sending a single, cryptic emoji
    - These animated ellipses have become so integral to the average American's sense of self-worth that their sudden unavailability could be catastrophic, causing broad-ranging devastation on par with that of climate change

What can you do?

- Count your dots!
    - Remember: An ellipsis consists of three dots, not two, not four (although a period followed by an ellipsis is acceptable in some cases); five is right out

    - You might ask, "If I use only two dots, won't that help conserve ellipses?"
        - No
        - Using two dots (or four or five) splits an ellipsis asunder, resulting in free radical dots
        - When these free radicals careen into nearby sentences, they may collide with other ellipses (or even colons, semicolons, question marks, exclamation points, or quotation marks), causing them to break apart, which could lead to a chain reaction that irrevocably alters punctuation as we know it
- Be judicious with your use of ellipses
    - Ask yourself, "Do I really need that ellipsis, or am I just using drama dots to create a false sense of importance in my writing?"
    - If any of your emails resemble the passage below, you may have contracted ellipsis overuse syndrome (EOS) and should seek grammatical help promptly

        Hello…Happy New Year…Let's hope that this one is better than the last…all things considered…

    - The ellipses in the above passage are not only unnecessary, but they are also perplexing and annoying
- If we all work together, we can save time and aggravation as we conserve ellipses for instances when they are truly needed!

FAQs

- What should I do if I have a friend or colleague with EOS?
    - Likely, the person doesn't realize they have a problem; direct confrontation could make them defensive and less amenable to advice
    - Instead, try leading by example: Dazzle them with your masterful use of commas, parentheses, and other punctuation so that they want to emulate you

- Is there a forum where I can report ellipses overuse to the authorities?
    - Government entities have no power to enforce conservation and appropriate use of ellipses
    - Thankfully, public shaming on the social media platform of your choice remains an option
- Aren't you getting a little bent out of shape about this? After all, they're only dots!
    - True, but when it comes down to it, aren't we all just made of dots?

My Biological Clock Needs a New Battery

I have never wanted to have children, but I've had a feeling for a while that I should want to have children. It's not because I feel it is my duty as a woman or anything like that, but rather that I feel that there must be some joy in it that I'm completely missing out on. Why else would people continue to have children in an age when contraceptives are so readily available? Everyone has always told me that I'll want children eventually, but I'm still waiting for those maternal instincts to kick in. I still feel so young, but I saw this report on the news the other day—scientist have determined that a woman's fertility begins to decline at the age of 27. Guess how old I am.

When I was younger, I used to tell people that I couldn't possibly consider having children until I could keep a plant alive. I've killed more plants than I can count. I've killed plants that you aren't supposed to be able to kill. I've killed a cactus! Who kills a cactus? Oh, but now I've kept my spider plant alive for over two years, and I've even given her a name (Guinivere). Does this mean I can't use the plant thing as an excuse for not having children anymore? I've even managed to keep a cat alive and well for almost a year now. Sure, I accidentally tripped over her twice last week, but she doesn't seem to be holding a grudge. But a cat is not a child. I couldn't leave a big dish of food and some water out for a child and go out of town for a few days. Children require so much more work, and I sometimes get afraid that I'm just too selfish to have kids.

I remember once a couple of years ago, I told my mother I wasn't sure if I wanted to have children. She gave me a smile that looked like it had been poured from a syrup bottle and said, "Oh, relax. I wasn't sure if I wanted kids when I was your age either." I did the math in my head. "Mom," I said, "you already had a child when you were my age." Her face fell. "Oh," she said. "I guess I meant that I didn't know if I wanted children when I was 19 or 20." Well, I'm not 19 anymore. I'm 27, and as I said earlier, scientists are now saying that my fertility is already declining. Damn scientists.

So, I think what I really want is to adopt a 20 year old. Pregnancy I want no part of. As it is now, I throw up in the morning when I'm just ovulating, so I can only imagine how awful the morning sickness will be. I won't even get into the mood swings, food cravings, weight gain, and general discomfort sure to come from carrying around another person. Childbirth I can do without too. I'm just not into pain. As for first steps, first teeth, first words, and bronzed baby shoes, all that sounds very sweet, but when you put all those things up against spitting up, crying, hundreds of diapers, temper tantrums, and runny noses—ugh! The thing that really depresses me, though, is the thought of being in my 50's and not having children. Who will I spend the holidays with? This is why, years down the road, I need to find some nice college student to adopt.

Of course, I know that will never work. So, I keep hoping that maybe my feelings will change. Perhaps someday I'll see a baby and think Yes, I want to have one of those! instead of No, I don't want to hold it. I might break it! Until then, I guess I'll stick to cats and plants. My mother just gave me an African violet last week, so I'll see how that goes.

My Valentine

"Erm, happy Valentine's Day?" Ian said dryly as he adjusted the stretchy gauze tape that prevented the ice packs from sliding off of my hands. I'd read that icing one's hands and feet during chemo infusions could help prevent neuropathy, so each week before my infusion began, we set up our icing protocol. In a basin, my feet rested on ice packs, and each foot had another pack placed on top of it. The stretchy tape helped secure ice packs to the backs of my hands, which I then positioned palms-down on top of packs that sat on each arm of my chair. I would endure the icing for as long as I could stand it, then I'd take a short break, and we'd set it all up again and repeat this cycle until my chemo session was finally over.

Years before, Ian and I had dispensed with exchanging gifts on Valentine's Day. We already had birthdays, Christmas, and our anniversary—those were more than enough. We'd also decided to avoid the crowds and pricey prix fixe menus at restaurants in favor of dinner dates (usually fondue) at home. Valentine's Day was nice, but we never made a big deal about it.

None of that meant I was thrilled about getting chemo on Valentine's Day, though. No one is ever thrilled about getting chemo, but sometimes it's a necessary evil. And so, it was on

Valentine's Day 2018. As he'd done for all of my chemo sessions so far (and would do for all those yet to come), Ian helped me with the ice packs and sat with me during the three to four hours it took to infuse the myriad chemicals into my veins. Some days, we'd be in the infusion center—a large room where eight treatment stations were sectioned off by curtains and surrounded the nurses' desk. On Valentine's Day, though, we had our own infusion room. It was spare and sterile, looking much like any doctor's office except for a recliner positioned where an exam table would typically be found, but it was private and much quieter than the infusion center. I sat in the recliner while Ian spent those hours in one of the rigid, non-reclining chairs in the room. I don't recall exactly how we passed the time that day. In all, I had sixteen treatments, and they tend to blur together in my mind. Sometimes we sat quietly and I almost managed to doze off, at least until a nurse came along to add the next drug to my IV. Other times, podcasts, music, or Mad Libs helped fill the hours. When the infusions were finally done, we'd pack up, Ian would drive us home, and we'd try not to think about the fact that we would have to do it all again in a week.

The worst of the chemo yuck usually hit me a day or two after the infusion, so while I still felt up to it, I liked to do what I could around the house in order to not feel totally useless. That night I made dinner. No fondue that day—that was too much work. Instead, I made chickpea burgers. As I formed them into heart shapes, I couldn't help but think they were the most romantic chickpea burgers ever.

It may not have been the most pleasant of Valentine's Days, but my heart swells as I think back on it. Sometimes love sweeps you off your feet with grand gestures and passionate declarations. But many times, it simply sits, dependably and reassuringly, by your side, helping you through the really hard stuff.

The Suffering Club

You'd think I would have understood the behavior of nine-year-old girls—after all, I was one myself. But no. As far as I could tell, there was no rhyme or reason to it. Had I been absent from school when the rules of being a preteen girl were explained? Or was I just supposed to intuit that being "best friends" with Jane one day didn't mean she wouldn't shun you the next day when you declined to trade your Oreos for her raisins? Then, somehow, before you knew it, every other girl in class followed suit and you were a pariah—all because you didn't want to make a crummy lunch deal.

My cohorts baffled me with their fickleness, sometimes downright cruelty. It was as if they were constantly examining me—and each other—for vulnerabilities, searching for that one thing, no matter how trivial, that was different. Once found, it could be exploited—prodded and picked at as needed to produce the desired effect. If I'd been living in the adult world, the fact that I didn't operate that way would have made me adequately non-sociopathic, perhaps even congenial. But I was in the cutthroat world of nine-year-old girls, so all it did was make me look desperate. In this world, to reject others was to elevate yourself. Anyone who can be so particular about her friends must be really cool, right? Perhaps there was a sort of logic to it, but it was one I didn't understand and felt helpless to navigate.

Despite the volatility of this societal microcosm, some girls—like Tracy and Amanda— managed to consistently inhabit its upper echelons. When I saw them approaching me one day at recess, something between thrill and panic stirred in my stomach.

"Do you want to join our club?" Amanda said, getting straight down to business.

A club? This was even better than I could have imagined. A club meant membership. It meant structure and rules, which might not be fair but at least would provide some guidance.

Knowing that eagerness was a sure sign of desperation, I tried to play it cool. Besides, after I'd had a couple of seconds to think, it sounded too good to be true. There had to be a catch. "What kind of club?" I did my best to sound just the right amount of uninterested.

"It's a club to show our devotion to Jesus," Tracy said.

I thought I was already a part of that club, being in Catholic school. But, of course, I couldn't say that. "What do you do?"

"It's called the Suffering Club," Amanda said. "Jesus suffered and died for us. We show Him devotion with our suffering."

This did not sound appealing at all, but I couldn't say that either. Doing so could mean not only being shunned but also being branded a Jesus hater. Anyhow, the suffering was probably for some greater good, like giving my allowance to charity instead of buying candy. I probably should have asked for more details, but my eagerness for a sense of belonging and security amid the grade school hellscape got the best of me. "Okay," I said.

"Good," said Amanda. "Every day, you'll get a suffering assignment."

Every day? In the brief time I'd even considered it, I had figured that any prescribed suffering would be weekly, or better yet, monthly. "What's today's?" I asked warily.

Tracy chewed thoughtfully on the ends of her hair. "We'll start you off easy. Instead of doing all your schoolwork during study period, you have to save some to do at home."

More than a couple of times, Tracy and Amanda had teased me, calling me a goody-goody for finishing all my work during school. This suffering task was obviously custom-made for me. Yes, many in the world had endured far worse, but I hated having homework if I could avoid it, especially on a practically perfect fall day with crisp air and warm sunshine mingling in perfect concert. There would be precious few of these days before winter descended, so I wanted to be outside after school, not behind a desk. Plus, later, there would be Thursday-night TV! Why let unnecessary homework throw a wrench in all that? It wasn't unbearable, but it seemed pointless. "Isn't there something else I could do?" I asked before I could stop myself. I knew the answer.

Amanda scoffed.

"I was just asking," I mumbled. People often say there's no harm in asking—a sound statement in most situations but not when you're dealing with nine-year-old girls. Forget sugar, spice, and everything nice. Venom, bile, and all things vile—that's what little girls are actually made of.

"Jesus died for you," Tracy said with a sneer. "Is having a little homework too much to ask?"

When she put it that way, it was hard to argue, except Jesus wasn't asking me. They were. And why? Maybe they'd just made up the whole Suffering Club thing to see what they could get me to do to gain their acceptance. "I don't see why Jesus would care."

"Suffering shows Jesus your devotion," Tracy said, "but I guess maybe you're not that devoted." Her voice was ripe with judgment.

"Guess what my assignment was today," Amanda said, daring me to guess.

I shrugged.

She proudly held up her palm and pulled back the Band-Aid on it. "I had to stick a safety pin into my hand." She paused, letting the drama percolate. "It's like the holes in Jesus' hands when he was crucified."

The mark on her palm was red—bigger and nastier than what you'd expect to get from a safety pin, but even so, comparing it to a crucifixion wound seemed like a stretch. Regardless, poking a pin into her hand for no good reason struck me as completely nuts. I'd like to think Jesus would've agreed.

Before I could respond, Amanda carefully replaced the Band-Aid on her self-inflicted stigmata. "I'm totally devoted to Jesus," she said smugly.

My stomach churned. I'd wanted to belong, and this was my chance. I'd wanted some simple rules I could follow to be accepted, and here they were being offered to me. But the rules didn't make sense, so would I really be any better off? "I don't get it," I said. "What good will any of this do?"

Tracy rolled her eyes and huffed. How dare I question a founder of the club! "This is how it works. It's our club. Are you in or not?"

Turning this down would be social suicide, at least until some other girl made a misstep and took my place as outcast of the moment. That could be as early as next week, but in third grade, a few days could seem like forever. But if I agreed to this, what would be next? Saving schoolwork for home and self-inflicted safety pin injuries might be preludes to fasting and self-flagellation. Already, I routinely gave up little bits of myself to fit in. Wasn't it enough that I often kept my hand down in class when I knew the answer to whatever question Miss Swanson was asking? I didn't want to seem too smart. Or what about the fact that I kept certain things I loved to myself—like the old jazz music my father played and reruns of M*A*S*H? It was better to just pretend to like whatever the cool kids were into. If those things weren't enough, what would be? Was enough even attainable?

Tracy and Amanda looked at me. They were waiting for my answer, but they weren't going to wait much longer.

I gulped and straightened my posture. "No thanks."

For a moment, they both look shocked, dumbfounded that anyone would turn down the chance to be in their club. But quickly, they composed themselves, turned their noses upward, and strode off together.

I never heard about the Suffering Club again. To this day, I don't know if it was real or just a ruse. I do know that if it was real, it had nothing to do with Jesus. Those girls suffered for one reason: to make themselves feel superior.

I still don't get it. And that's probably for the best.

Thought for Food

Food as life: You are what you eat.

Food as death: Those double bacon cheeseburgers'll kill ya.

Food as reward: I ran five miles today. I deserve that sundae, damn it!

Food as entertainment: I'm bored. I wonder if anything interesting is going on in the refrigerator.

Food as art: I have had meals that were almost too pretty to eat. Almost.

Food as enemy: Oh, chocolate chip cookies, why do you look even more appealing when I want to lose a few pounds? Evil bastards!

Food as anxiety: I have three lasagnas for ten people. Do you think that's enough? Maybe I should get some more bread.

Food as condolence: The refrigerator of a grieving family is seldom empty as people offer their sympathies with casseroles and salads.

Food as memory: I can still hear the sound of the old-fashioned crank coffee grinder that my dad used to grind wheat for Sunday morning pancakes.

Food as belief: Stale cracker or body of Christ? The answer is in the mouth of the beholder.

Food as incentive: No dessert for you unless you finish your brussels sprouts!

Food as love: I cut a piece of homemade banana bread for my husband and bring it to him at his desk while it's still warm. In turn, when there are only a couple of pieces remaining, he takes the end and leaves me a middle piece because he knows I like those better.

Food as artillery: Food fight!

Food as commiseration: Girlfriends bonding over a pan of "men are pigs" brownies.

Food as change: Summer salads make way for hearty stews as the leaves on the trees change color.

Food as apology: I'm sorry my dog dug up your prize azaleas… I made muffins!

Food as anathema: It was called salmon loaf, and the thought of it still makes me shudder. Unless starvation is otherwise imminent, only cats should be served fish that has been canned and then pressed into a mold.

Food as sedative: Post-Thanksgiving dinner nap, anyone?

Food as celebration: Happy birthday to me! And to you! And to everyone! Let's have cake!

What I Really Want to Write in my Query Letter

Dear Literary Agent:

Normally, this is where I would tell you I'm seeking representation for my novel and explain why I am spending several of the finite number of minutes I have left on this earth writing a query letter to you, but, honestly, I don't see why I should bother.

I'm not one of those inexplicable celebrities who, through some ouroboric twist of fate, is famous for being famous. Thus, I can offer you no memoir full of meretricious drivel to distract readers from the gaping voids in their lives or their existential dread. Likewise, I have not surrendered my common sense, integrity, and/or soul to work under (thankfully now former) President Fuckface and subsequently write a tell-all screed about the myriad behind-the-scenes horrors of that administration.

My trilogy of fan fiction novels filled with laughably atrocious prose that glorifies abusive relationships will not be rocketing up the bestseller list with baffling rapidity—because I have not written said books. I do not claim to hold the secrets to manifesting longevity and financial success via positive thinking. I have not compiled a text filled with narcissistic optimism disguised as folksy wisdom explaining how to work fewer hours and enjoy life more by being born into wealth and exploiting the less fortunate. I have not devised a series of foolproof weight-loss plans based on a combination of the dieter's astrological sign, eye color, and middle name.

Alas, all I have to offer is a well-written, engaging story with interesting, sympathetic characters. On the off chance you might be looking for something like that, I have included my sample pages below.

Cynically yours,
Elizabeth Barton

BIBLIOGRAPHY

Works in this anthology that were first published elsewhere are listed below in (roughly) chronological order:

WOW: Women on Writing, www.wow-womenonwriting.com, Quarterly Flash Fiction Contest, Spring 2009

- *The Wedding March*

—, Summer 2009

- *Not Tonight*

Skirt! magazine, Morris Communications, November 2009

- *The Kid Question*

This City Bus, Neighborhood Writing Alliance, *Journal of Ordinary Thought*, Summer 2010

- *Waking*

Gemini magazine, gemini-magazine.com, October 2010

- *Three Minutes*

Water on Fire, Neighborhood Writing Alliance, *Journal of Ordinary Thought*, Fall 2010

- *The Sign*

I Always Like Plenty of Napkins, Neighborhood Writing Alliance, *Journal of Ordinary Thought*, Winter 2011

- *Thought for Food*

Flashlight Memories, Silver Boomer Books, 2011

- *The Little Blue Book*

Nil Desperandum, ndstories.com, April 2011

- *Regarding Emma*

Shell and Yolk, Neighborhood Writing Alliance, *Journal of Ordinary Thought*, Spring 2011

- *Dear Writer's Block*

Testify, Neighborhood Writing Alliance, *Journal of Ordinary Though*, Summer 2011

- *The Elephant on the Lawn*

Bylines 2012 Desk Calendar. Snowflake Press, 2012

- *A List of Possible Reasons That More of My Work Has Not Yet Been Published*

I Believed Every Word, Neighborhood Writing Alliance, *Journal of Ordinary Thought*, Winter 2012

- *A Host of Problems*

The Open Gate, Neighborhood Writing Alliance, *Journal of Ordinary Thought*, Spring 2012

- *Dear Anne*

When We Listen, Neighborhood Writing Alliance, *Journal of Ordinary Thought*, Winter 2012

- *Just Be Happy!*
- *To the Unconceived*

In This Place, Neighborhood Writing Alliance, *Journal of Ordinary Thought*, Spring 2013

- *Sister*

You Don't Know Us. Budlong Woods Writers, DPOETRAE Productions, 2016

- *Down There*
- *Paradox*
- *Tabula Rasa*

Monsters, Myths, and Other Matters, Budlong Woods Writers, DPOETRAE Productions, 2017

- *Dear Len*
- *Four Days in November*

Tchotchkes, Budlong Woods Writers, DPOETRAE Productions 2019

- *The Ballad of Belle Gunness*
- *Crossroads?*
- *How Are You?*
- *I Am From*
- *The Joy of Socks*

Prime Number magazine, www.press53.com/prime-number-magazine-index, issue 173, 2020

- *Endurance*

50 Give or Take #1, Vine Leaves Press, 2021

- *Excavation* (#183)

50-Word Stories, fiftywordstories.com, May 2021

- *Overzealous*
- *Bountiful Harvest*

Every Day Fiction, everydayfiction.com, May 2021

- *Suckers!*

Love, Death, and Everything in Between, Budlong Woods Writers, DPOETRAE *Productions*, 2021

- *Better*
- *The Ballad of Herman Mudgett*
- *Memento*
- *My Valentine*

Intrinsick magazine, www.intrinsick.com, July 2021

- *Pith and Pretense*

Defenestration magazine, www.defenestrationmag.net, August 2021

- *The Definitive Guide to Writing the Perfect Query Letter*

Borrowed Solace magazine, borrowedsolace.com, issue 4.2, 2021

- *The Night Watch*

50 Give or Take #2, Vine Leaves Press, 2022

- *The Beginning of the End of the Line* (#590)
- *Changing with the Times* (#624)
- *First Impression* (#477)
- *Goodbye, Girls* (#547)
- *I Want to Break Free* (#497)
- *Misspelling* (#613)
- *Ontogeny* (#423)
- *Suspension* (#371)

Points in Case, www.pointsincase.com, March 2021

- *Mind Your Dots: A Public Service Announcement on the Responsible Use of Ellipses*

101 Words, 101words.org, April 2022

- *Deathright*

—, 101words.org, July2022

- *Found and Lost*

Manawaker Studio's Flash Fiction Podcast, www.manawaker.com/podcast, April 2022

- *Duped*

—, February 2023

- *Leave No Trace*

The Arcanist, thearcanist.io, November 2022

- *Lullaby*

Dream: n. Hope; Aspiration; Ambition, Budlong Woods Writers, DPOETRAE Productions, 2023

- A *Brief Bio Statement for Query Letters to Literary Agents*
- *Dream Players*
- *Not a Morning Person*
- *Requiem*
- *Unsung*

ACKNOWLEDGEMENTS

The author would like to thank the purveyors of the many online publications and contests for providing creative outlets and the incentive to continually develop new stories. Particular thanks goes to the editors of the publications listed in the Bibliography for actually accepting some of these pieces and sharing them with the world.

Thanks also to the members of the Neighborhood Writers Alliance and Budlong Woods Writers for all of their advice, critiques, support, and encouragement over the years.

And special thanks to all my family, friends, and colleagues who provided the resources, space, and encouragement to write, write, and then write some more.

About the Author

Elizabeth Ott Barton (1974-2022) was born in Milwaukee and raised in Fredonia, Wisconsin where she developed a love for storytelling at an early age. After studying at Bradley University and the University of Illinois at Urbana-Champaign, she settled in Chicago with her husband Ian and various cats, cultivating a love for food & libations, travel, and a hobby of collecting hobbies. Her work appeared in anthologies published by the Neighborhood Writing Alliance, the Budlong Woods Writers, and various collections of flash/micro fiction. She was also the author of two novels, *The Amber of the Moment* and *Unfinished Business*.

www.ingramcontent.com/pod-product-compliance
Lightning Source LLC
Chambersburg PA
CBHW031252170626
46807CB00001B/107

9798988045441